D0860124

the Miracle Stealer

the MIRACLE STEALER

NEIL CONNELLY

ARTHUR A. LEVINE BOOKS *An Imprint of Scholastic Inc.*

Connelly, Neil O.
The miracle stealer / Neil Connelly. — 1st ed.
p. cm.
Summary: In small-town Pennsylvania, nineteen-year-old Andi Grant will do anything to protect her six-year-old brother Daniel from those who believe he has a God-given gift as a healer — including their own mother.
ISBN 978-0-545-13195-7 (hardcover : alk. paper) [1. Healers — Fiction. 2. Miracles — Fiction. 3. Brothers and sisters — Fiction. 4. Faith — Fiction. 5. Camps — Fiction. 6. Family life — Pennsylvania — Fiction. 7. Pennsylvania — Fiction.] I. Title.
PZ7.C76186Mir 2010
[Fic] — dc22

2010000727

10 9 8 7 6 5 4 3 2 1 10 11 12 13 14

Printed in the U. S. A. 23

First edition, October 2010

For Owen and James,
the only proof I'll ever need

CHAPTER ONE

I needed to save Daniel. That's why I made the choices I did. I didn't need for my dad to come home, and I didn't need for my mother and me to have some grand reconciliation. I didn't need the track scholarships I'd turned down or the futures they promised. I didn't even need Jeff Cedars to fall in love with me a second time. All I needed was for my kid brother to have a normal life, and I believed with all my heart that I knew the way to give it to him. The only problem, as I came to find out, was that just believing something doesn't make it true.

Take for example what some believe about the morning that ragged rescue crew pulled baby Daniel from the earth after three days buried alive. I suppose that like most of the planet you watched on TV, saw his body strapped to that board, his cheeks bloodied and his eyes blinking in the day's first light. You heard the word whispered reverently by every wide-eyed reporter: *miracle*. Afterward, some people couldn't get enough of that crazy story. They took it as gospel truth that Daniel died in that hole and came back to life as something more, something better. In no time the tabloids and nutjob websites filled with wild rumors about my brother, about the fire that didn't burn him and the cripples he cured and the blind whose eyes he opened. But the thing about stories like Daniel's is that they take on a life of their own. Nobody really knows what happened for sure except the ones who saw it all firsthand, like I did.

In the hospital, right at the end of the life I used to lead, Leo told me that seeing something happen only makes you an observer. To qualify as a witness, he explained, you have to offer testimony, share your own truth with others. So I'll tell you all I saw and did, plain as I can, and you'll decide for yourself just what to believe about the Miracle Boy of Paradise, Pennsylvania. I'll start with the Saturday night about a year back, a midsummer evening when, if you trust the rumors, my brother Daniel walked across the waters of Paradise Lake to bring a baby girl back from the dead.

After midnight I was in my bed down in Cabin Two, but I was wide awake, alert, and waiting. I knew from Gayle that Mrs. Abernathy was close. When the screen door of the main house creaked open and snapped shut, I rolled from my bed, knelt by my window, and brushed back the worn curtain. Up the hill and beyond the dark columns of trees, I could see my mother crossing through the yellow porch light and down the stone steps. She led Daniel by the wrist. With his free hand he was rubbing at his eyes.

Already dressed, I jammed on my sneakers and took off through my living room, out onto my porch, and then up the steep trail, ducking beneath hairy hemlock arms and scraping against the rough bark of pines. By the time I got to the truck, my mother had tossed Daniel into his booster and strapped the seat belt across his chest. I reached for the passenger door handle, but she fisted down the lock. Our eyes met through the window. Daniel, wide-eyed and startled, was wearing the Batman pajamas

I'd just bought him for his sixth birthday. He looked tired and confused. My mother straightened and turned the key, causing the engine to sputter to life and the tailpipe to cough smoke. But before she could pull away, I charged right into the headlights and slammed both hands on the hood. We stared at each other through the dirty windshield until her face soured and she cranked down her window. "They called," she said.

I looked at Daniel. "Little Man, open that door and hop on out."

He glanced toward my mother but otherwise stayed frozen.

My hands shivered from the engine's hum. My mother gripped the steering wheel. "The Abernathys are good people," she said, "and they need our help. Can't you try to have a little faith?"

"I got all the faith I need. Faith in Bert and Dr. Ghadari. Mr. Abernathy needs to call the hospital."

"You know how they feel after what happened last time. That's not our decision."

"It's not our decision to keep Daniel safe? Look at your son, Ma."

Tears were slipping down his freckled cheeks now, and he was running a hand through his short blond crew cut.

My mother shook her head. "He's crying because you upset him. He was fine before you came and got him all riled up. He wants to go and help. It's a sin not to use the gifts God gives you."

I looked at my brother and remembered his fevered face the night Mrs. Bundower died. And when the elders of our church — a pack of four-star loonies — accused him of not praying hard enough after the fish kill that same summer, I was the one who found him alone in his bed, sweaty and trembling as he tried to do the impossible. I leaned my chest down into the grille and locked my knees out behind me, as if I could halt the truck like one of the superheroes in the comic books Daniel loved. "Daniel's not praying for anybody tonight," I told my mother.

Daniel sniffled and wiped tears from his face. "Everybody's yelling. I was dreaming 'bout a red balloon."

"There's no time for this," my mother shouted. She shifted into gear and locked eyes with me again. It seemed entirely likely that she might run me down, but I didn't budge. "Fine," she finally said, "come with us if you must."

I stepped out of the headlights' shine. Just as I rounded the bumper, the truck surged forward, spitting up rocks and dust. I smacked the rear quarter panel and saw Daniel spin around in the seat, tugging against the restraint. He watched me through the rear window. His freckled cheeks and wet, brown eyes grew smaller and smaller as the truck curved down our driveway. The brakes, long past their prime, whined in protest, and then the headlights swung right onto Roosevelt Road.

I kicked at the gravel and cursed, then glanced at the crescent moon. It was a fingernail in the cloudless sky, not casting enough light to run by. But I bent quick and tied the laces of my sneakers, pictured the blisters I'd get from jogging without socks, then took off down the trail. Because of the Black Hole, I knew my mother would need to drive south and swing below the dam before heading north again on the far side of the lake. If I made good time running straight north and had a little luck, I might beat her to the Abernathys'.

And so I ran, down past my log cabin and Cabins Three and Four, then past the brick chimney rising from the charred square of earth where Cabin Five used to be, back before my dad left Paradise behind. I'd jogged the path along the shoreline a thousand times, and my feet were quick to find the safe pace I could travel in the half-light. I focused on planting my feet cleanly on the roots and rocks and pine needles, pumping my arms, breathing easy. In darkness, I passed through the compounds that once belonged to the Marshalls and the Zanines and the MacKenns, all of them gone, and the guest cabins they once rented out now falling apart — shattered windows and cobwebbed porches.

Back when I was a kid, the lake was crowded with people all summer long. From Memorial Day to Labor Day, every Friday found Roosevelt Road hosting a parade of fathers delivering their families to Paradise in gleaming station wagons. I used to love meeting the guests, making quick friends, showing them around the compound that Dad and I tended as a team. When I was ten, we raked leaves into piles and burned them together, repainted the interiors of the cabins side by side. At twelve, I helped him mow and he taught me the proper use of every tool in his toolbox, one by one. Sure, people called me a tomboy, but that was nothing new for a short-haired girl with a man's name. By thirteen, I was next to Dad, dipping my chain saw into the trees that dropped in the winter storms. On the night I'm telling you about now, I was nineteen, and by that point, I was taking care of things around the compound pretty much on my own.

I broke from the forest into the open field of Roosevelt Park, and the stars spread over the whole dome of the sky, beautiful and bright. With that bit of extra light and a path free of roots and rocks, I sped up to my normal pace and then beyond. As I crossed the grass, I felt that weird tug from the forest above the picnic pavilions. Up that slope are the shale walls stacked by settlers two centuries ago, and the wild apple orchard where Jeff Cedars and I used to take long walks and spend time alone. Beyond that is the fairy fort.

Midway across the open field I passed the bronze statue of Franklin Delano Roosevelt, who came up with the great idea of building a dam at the southern end of Paradise Valley to create a man-made lake and generate electricity. That was 1932, so most of the people who lived in the low country were happy to take the buyout money, but one family refused. Irene McGinley and her two sons had come from Ireland on a steamer late in the nineteenth century, and to show the good Lord their appreciation for safe passage to the New World, they built a fine church with a steeple next to their home along the banks of the Lackawaxen River. The day the Civilian Conservation Corps finally blocked the flow of the river, Mrs. McGinley lashed herself and her boys to the bell tower of the church and cursed the town as the waters rose and drowned them. So the story goes.

Decades later, some folks started hearing the church bell late at night, tolling out from under the lake. They claimed it was an omen, that if you heard it, then trouble was coming your way. The mothers of Paradise began warning their children, "Be home by dark, or Mrs. McGinley might call you to her church at the bottom of the lake." When little Gabriella Abernathy fell through the ice, and just a year later, when Mrs. Abernathy miscarried at the hospital, the curse was clearly at work. Mrs. McGinley was judged responsible for the great ice storm that trashed the whole town and the fire that torched Cabin Five (though there's at least one thing she can't take credit for). And later when all the fish died overnight, nearly all the crazies agreed it was due to the old woman's wrath.

For the longest time, back when I was a child, I believed. In Mrs. McGinley and the Easter Bunny and saying your prayers at night to Jesus and all the things your parents tell you. I was one of those oddball kids who actually liked going to church.

I left the park, passing beneath the tattered banner strung across the main entrance — CELEBRATE PARADISE DAYS! — and followed Roosevelt Road into town. I avoided the fractured sidewalks and jogged down the middle of the street, past the courthouse and Jorvik's Sporting Man's Store with the plywood nailed over the windows and Killarney's Antiques and Used Books with its stacks of dusty paperbacks. I passed the cramped offices of the *Five Mountains Gazetteer*, the local weekly paper where I worked part-time, mostly writing obituaries and pretending I was getting valuable experience for my career as a journalist.

The road dipped as I neared the bridge, and without breaking stride, I hurdled the guardrail they'd planted across the entrance and passed the signs warning DANGER! NO PEDESTRIAN CROSSING. I shifted to the right and slowed. In the weak moonlight, I couldn't really see the road beneath my feet. It was like I was running across the open air.

When I reached the Black Hole, dead center in the middle of the bridge, I slowed even more, enough to peek through to the gurgling rapids below. Fifty feet below me, the river fed into the lake. A chunk of asphalt about the size of a man had fallen away during the great ice storm three years before, and the state engineers had declared that the bridge would have to be torn down and rebuilt. But with the fish gone and Paradise on the decline, funds were tight, so they hung up those warning signs and put the project on perpetual hold. Meanwhile, that hole got bigger and bigger, and by now a car could easily have tumbled through. The safe passage was only a few feet on either side, and I picked my way carefully along the railing.

Roosevelt Road rises sharply on the west side of the bridge, and I had to lean forward into the incline. Though I was breathing hard, as the ground leveled out I tapped into what Coach Halloran always called my sixth gear, an extra reserve of sweet energy I saved for the end of a race. All through my high school track meets, I was usually in second place coming into the final stretch, but more often than not, my chest was the one snapping the ribbon. The recruiter from Lock Haven University, the same guy I spoke to about deferring my scholarship, told me that was the difference between a good runner and a great one, that ability to finish strong.

So when I again entered the forest and the road veered south, I was virtually in an all-out sprint, barreling down a long canopy made by the pines. I kept expecting to see the headlights of my mother's truck appear in the darkness, but they never did. When I finally reached the Abernathys' property, I didn't see our truck in the long driveway, and I felt a rush of victory.

I charged through their side yard, dominated by the towering Grandfather Elm, supposedly huge even before they built this Victorian mansion. But when I rounded that ancient tree, I saw my mother's pickup, parked crooked halfway into a flower bed, headlights shining, engine running, like she'd crashed into the garden. The truck was empty. I took the porch steps two at a time, shouldered through the double doors, and found myself suddenly inside the darkened house, facing a long wooden staircase. At the top, a dim light glowed. I sprinted up the stairs and then down a hallway toward an open door and the lighted room at the end, and I was going full tilt when I reached the threshold, but what I saw nailed my feet to the floor.

Directly ahead of me, propped up on her canopy bed, Mrs. Abernathy sat naked from the chest down. The skin of her pregnant belly stretched tight. Blood stained the sheets between her open legs, and even now I don't think there's any right way to label what I saw there, but at the time the word that came to me was *wound*. By nineteen I knew plenty about the pain and bloody burden of being a woman, but in that crazy frozen moment, what I saw seemed foreign and impossible, unnatural.

I heard my name and turned to my mother, kneeling alongside the bed with Daniel. "Anderson," my mother repeated. She stared at the hardwood next to her. "Now you see for yourself. Come pray with us."

Daniel was much calmer than he'd been in the truck. I studied his face for signs of distress, but found nothing. He looked completely unsurprised by my appearance. "Hey, Andi," he said with a half smile. "That baby's coming."

In a daze, I wandered closer, looked at the open space meant for me, but I did not kneel. Mr. Abernathy sat on the other side of the bed, cradling his wife's head. People said she had lost her mind after the death of her second child. For a couple months, she went to stay at a hospital out west, and when she came back, you never saw her without her husband at her side. When she talked to you, her eyes didn't quite settle on yours. She was always looking over your shoulder, like somebody else was watching.

From the bathroom, Sylvia Volpe appeared, striding across the room on her long crane legs. Volpe was an outsider, a white-haired writer who had moved to Paradise because she couldn't get enough of Daniel's story. Before that, she worked for one of those newspapers sold at the grocery checkout lane with promises of miracle diets and the mysteries of Atlantis revealed. Volpe contributed less fantastic stories now and then to the *Gazetteer*, but if we ran into each other in the office, we didn't speak. She handed Mr. Abernathy a wet facecloth, then aimed her sharp chin my way. "You have no place here," she said.

"Go get abducted by an alien," I snapped back.

My mother sighed. "Stop it, the both of you."

Sweat beaded across Mrs. Abernathy's pale face, and her husband dabbed at it with the cloth. Her eyes were closed and her lips were barely parted. I couldn't tell if breath was passing through them or not. Mr. Abernathy rubbed the cloth against her neck and whispered, "He's here now, Grace, just like you wanted. Can you feel him? The boy's right here with us."

Below me, my mother and Daniel bent their heads into the mattress to pray.

"We should bring Daniel downstairs," I told my mother. "He shouldn't be here now." All I could think of was Mrs. Bundower and the raspy suck of air and the way the skin on her face pulled back so tight it looked like a skull.

"This is precisely where he belongs," Volpe said. She straightened her gold-rimmed glasses. "This is the place to which Jesus has called him." She always sounded like whatever she was saying she had on personal authority from Jesus, like she had a holy private number on her cell phone's speed dial.

I put a hand on Daniel's shoulder and was about to speak, but a low moan from Mrs. Abernathy stopped me. Slowly her fingers gripped the bedsheets, gathering handfuls into tight fists. Her head pressed back into the pillow and her back arched, bent knees trembling in the air, and when her mouth opened wide, the sound that ripped loose was more roar than scream. Her whole body heaved and shook, like someone possessed by a demon. Mr. Abernathy stood and pressed his hands onto her convulsing shoulders. "What's wrong? This shouldn't be happening. There's too much blood, Sylvia. We should do something."

But Volpe shook her head. "No. Her spirit's strong. And Daniel's here now. We have to believe." Again she stared at my brother, still kneeling.

"Daniel," I said. "Come on with me." I took a few steps toward the door, hoping he'd just follow. But when I looked back from the doorway, the face he aimed at me over his shoulder was blank. He didn't look scared or upset. If anything, perhaps he was disappointed.

"Maybe we better all stay here," Daniel said.

Mrs. Abernathy's convulsions eased, and Volpe extended both her lanky arms over the trembling body. She raised her face to the bed's white canopy and said, "Join with me now."

My mother got off her knees and took one of Daniel's hands, urging him to his feet, and Mr. Abernathy stood. The four of them joined hands, then Volpe and my mother both offered me their open hands, waiting for me to complete the prayer chain. My mother said, "Please, Ann." But I stayed where I was and shook my head. Volpe slid her palm into my mother's, and they turned from me. Looking heavenward, Volpe said, "Merciful Christ, Father in heaven, giver of life, we place our trust in you. We join together in hope and faith."

Mrs. Abernathy's moans started getting louder, and her lips spread back to reveal her clenched teeth. Mr. Abernathy shouted above her, "Please Jesus!"

"Thy will!" Volpe shouted. "Deliver us this night. Amen, amen."

My mother chanted, "Yes, Lord," over and over, swaying her body and rolling her head. Daniel still looked okay, but I knew that wouldn't last. I scanned the room and found a phone on a table by an open window. I crossed behind Volpe, and at the window I could see the lake through the trees.

When I reached for the receiver, Mr. Abernathy cried out, "Don't! You can't!"

"You need to take Daniel downstairs," I hollered at my mother. "Like right now."

"Put down that phone," Volpe ordered.

"It's not what she'd want," Mr. Abernathy yelled. "Not after last time."

Turning from all of them, I faced the lake and the crescent moon. I dialed 9-1-1. The familiar voice answered on the first ring, and with all the shouting behind me I had to practically scream, "Bert, it's Andi Grant. We need the ambulance up at the Abernathys' place. Hurry, Bert."

"No!" Mr. Abernathy yelled, and the anger in his voice mixed with Volpe's prayer and my mother's rising chant. But somehow in that crash of sounds we all heard Mrs. Abernathy when she whispered, "Don't need . . . any doctors." Mrs. Abernathy's body stilled and her eyes opened. She turned her weary face to Daniel and said faintly, "Only him."

The dial tone sounded in my ear, and I put the phone down. When I looked again, my brother was climbing up onto the bed, leaning back into the pile of pillows with Mrs. Abernathy. Her pale face twitched, as if something were coming alive beneath the skin, and she began panting, slowly at first and then more quickly. Mr. Abernathy, Volpe, and my mother closed the prayer circle and squeezed one another's hands, a trinity of true believers. Mrs. Abernathy bit her lip and turned her wet red face to my brother.

Daniel said, "Your tiny girl, she's afraid."

"What?"

"That baby. She's afraid to come out. Everybody's yelling. She's scared."

Mrs. Abernathy laughed but then her face turned serious. "I'm scared too, Daniel. And it hurts. Please. Daniel. Won't you intercede?"

Daniel smoothed the sweaty hair from her forehead. "When I was little, my daddy used to sing me a song when I was sad or scared."

At the mention of my father, my mother stiffened, but she didn't look at me and I didn't look at her.

Daniel's head began to nod to a rhythm only he could hear, and then he started to sing, "*There was a hole, in the middle of the ground, the prettiest hole, that you ever did see. And the green grass grew all around all around and the green grass grew all around.*"

Mrs. Abernathy eased her head back into the pillow and

stared straight up into the canopy of her bed. Her chest rose and fell as she took one deep breath, then another. I hadn't heard that song in years, but of course, I remembered it too, in my father's voice, husky but gentle.

As Daniel began the second verse, my mother joined in. *"And in that hole, there was a tree, the prettiest tree, that you ever did see. And the tree in the hole and the hole in the ground, and the green grass grew all around all around and the green grass grew all around."*

Mrs. Abernathy's fingers released the bunched-up sheets and worked their way into the hands of her husband on one side and my mother on the other. Now she was a link in the prayer chain. Daniel and my mother sang together, *"And in that tree, there was a branch, the prettiest branch, that you ever did see."*

Mr. Abernathy choked back tears and added his deep, cracking voice to the chorus, *"And the branch on the tree and the tree in the hole and the hole in the ground, and the green grass grew all around all around and the green grass grew all around."*

"It's coming now," Mrs. Abernathy whispered.

"Steady her knees," Volpe said, pulling her hands free of the prayer chain. My mother took hold of Mrs. Abernathy's one knee and I took hold of the other. The flesh was hot. I tried not to look at the wound.

Meanwhile, Daniel kept right on singing. *"And on that branch, there was a nest, the prettiest nest, that you ever did see."*

And now all of us, Daniel and Mr. Abernathy and my mother and Volpe and, yes, even me, we all sang. *"And the nest on the branch and the branch on the tree and the tree in the hole and the hole in the ground, and the green grass grew all around all around and the green grass grew all around."*

Volpe said, "Push now, Grace. Push!" She held her open hands at the wound, and when I looked down, a hard round shape emerged, a wet stone swirled with hair. Volpe said, "I see the head."

Mrs. Abernathy screamed, just once, and Daniel sang gently, *"And in the nest, there was an egg, the prettiest egg, that you ever did see."*

Afraid to stop now, we all sang with him. *"And the egg in the nest and the nest on the branch and the branch on the tree and the tree in the hole and the hole in the ground, and the green grass grew all around all around and the green grass grew all around."*

An entire tiny face, purple-gray, slimy and scrunched up, appeared suddenly from the wound. Its little bird eyes were closed, and it made no sound. I knew that when babies are born they're supposed to be crying, so that silence was awful, the worst thing I ever heard.

Volpe placed her hands on either side of the baby's slick head. She whispered, "Please, Jesus. No."

The room went totally quiet except for Mrs. Abernathy's breathing, louder and faster than even my own after a race. Everyone was looking at Volpe, who sat on the stool holding the head of the still child, apparently unsure what to do next. Nobody but me was looking at Daniel. He closed his eyes and dipped his head. I saw his lips moving quick, forming words no one could hear. His face turned a shade whiter and a bead of sweat rolled down one cheek. And I saw his chin begin to quiver and his eyes roll beneath their lids, like a convulsion was about to possess him. I stepped forward to grab my brother, snap him out of this insane fantasy, but he opened his eyes and smiled. I smelled something like vanilla suddenly in the air, and before I could recall where I'd encountered the scent before, Daniel, sweet Daniel, finished his song all by himself. *"And in that egg, there was a chick, the prettiest chick, that you ever did see. And the chick in the egg and the egg in the nest and the nest on the branch and the branch on the tree and the tree in the hole and the hole in the ground, and the green grass grew all around all around and the green grass grew all around."*

At the instant Daniel finished, that child blinked its blue eyes twice. And it was like staring into the clearest summer sky, that's how deep those blue eyes seemed. With a sploosh, the baby squirted from the wound, and Volpe caught it and wrapped it in a green towel. She offered the squirming bundle up to Mrs. Abernathy, whose hands stretched down to take her daughter. "She's all right?" Mrs. Abernathy asked.

"Everything's okay," Daniel answered. His face looked normal again. And with that the child opened its mouth and its crying echoed off the high walls. It was a healthy wail and everyone in the room except for Daniel began to sniffle, and maybe I cried a little too.

From the open window, I heard a second wailing, the siren of the ambulance circling the lake on Roosevelt Road. Everyone turned to the sound. The baby's crying quieted as she nuzzled in to her mom's neck.

"Praise Him," Mrs. Abernathy said. "Praise God for touching Daniel, making him His holy instrument here on earth."

Now I was still feeling pretty relieved that the baby had been born okay. But these words, they fell on me like mighty rocks dropped from heaven. I'm not going to pretend I knew then everything that was going to happen. I didn't. But that bad feeling I'd had lying in my cabin settled again in my gut, and I walked away from Mrs. Abernathy's bed over to the open window. Red and white strobing lights flickered through the forest on the far side of Paradise Lake, and behind the distant siren's cry, I thought I heard something else, slow and deep and rhythmic, like the clanging of some terrible bell.

CHAPTER TWO

My mother left us by ourselves on the first floor of St. Jude's Regional Medical Center. The visitors' area was a square box of a room with no windows and a TV hanging precariously from the ceiling in one corner, broadcasting static. Despite the NO SMOKING signs, the gray taste of cigarettes hung in the stale air. For ten minutes I stood on one of the mismatched chairs and tried to tune in something other than fuzz, but finally I gave up and settled down next to Daniel. He was flipping through the same coverless comic book he'd been looking at during the afternoon ride up from Paradise. The comic came from a bundle I'd bought him at a flea market over in Hawley, ten for a dollar. On the page spread across his lap, Superman sat alone in his Fortress of Solitude, an icy castle he hid in at the North Pole when the burden of saving the world got to be too much for him.

"I need a Crunch bar," Daniel announced, looking over at the snack machines. This was his third request.

"You don't need it. You want it," I told him.

"Okay. I want a Crunch bar."

"You didn't have lunch yet," I said. "Besides, I'm not paying a buck fifty for a candy bar."

"But I'm hungry."

"You're only hungry because there's candy in front of you. Don't look at it."

With an annoyed sigh, he went back to Superman. From the way Daniel was acting, I was pretty sure he didn't remember the last time we were here, how I found him huddled up in that broom closet after Mrs. Bundower died, squeezing his fat fingers in prayer and sucking back tears. It had been three years ago, after all — half his lifetime.

While Daniel and I waited, my mother had gone upstairs to check with the Abernathys to see if this was still an okay time to visit with them and the baby, now two days old but still nameless. I felt certain she was up there warning them that I'd come along, which certainly wasn't part of the agreed-upon plan. Everyone would worry that my heathen presence would somehow infect the innocent child.

When I was just six, Grandpa Anderson, the man I was named after and the original owner of the Camp Anderson compound, died in this very building. So hospitals have been near the top of my list of things I absolutely hate for a long time. The past year of my life hasn't done much to change this. But that day I swallowed my fear of white coats and hypodermic needles for Daniel's sake. I didn't trust my mother any more than she trusted me.

"Hey, Andi," Daniel said, "if Superman and Jesus had a battle, who'd win?" He didn't lift his face from the comic.

"Superman and Jesus are both good guys," I said. "They wouldn't fight."

Daniel turned a page. "But what if they did? What if Lex Luthor brainwashed Superman and made him evil and he was knocking down a church or something. You think Jesus could stop him?"

I pictured Jesus holding a green chunk of Kryptonite, standing over a genuflecting but still-undefeated Man of Steel. I knew that Jesus preached peace and love, but He went nuts in the temple that one time, so I figured He had a good fight in Him. Strange, but I always liked Jesus better when He was acting more like a person and less like a god.

"Superman's make-believe," I told Daniel. "You know that."

"Sure, I know. And Jesus is for real. Right?"

I was quiet. Though he was just six, Daniel had a way of asking things like this all the time, and you never got used to it. It wasn't just "Do fish get colds?" or "What happens to the sun at night?" He wanted to know if people had their own beds in heaven, why God made villains, where the angels in his dreams went when he was awake. This curiosity made him seem old and wise, despite his innocent brown eyes, despite the freckles that spotted both cheeks. When he was little, I would pretend to count those freckles, telling him each one was from an angel's kiss.

Picking up on my hesitation, Daniel repeated, "Right?" Now he was looking deep into my face. Explaining my thoughts on Superman was a lot easier than explaining my thoughts on Jesus, which had changed quite a bit over the years. Besides, why would I share my doubts and complicate his perfect faith?

I stood up and crossed to the doorway. The hall was empty, just shiny tiles and an abandoned gurney. Over the loudspeaker, a voice asked Dr. Armstrong to report to Radiology. There was a Code 76.

I turned back to my brother. "If Lex Luthor brainwashed Superman into being evil and Jesus showed up, he'd unbrainwash him back into his normal self and they wouldn't have to fight."

Daniel considered my solution and nodded his head. "Awesome." He folded up the comic book and set it on the cushion where I'd been sitting. "Hey, Andi, how come there aren't any fish in the fish tank?" He hopped down and walked over to an aquarium set in the wall beneath the staticky TV. I hadn't noticed the absence of fish until Daniel pointed it out, and even when I joined him for a closer inspection, we couldn't see any signs of life in the murky water. I wondered if they got the water from Paradise Lake, a thought that made me scan the surface for floaters.

"Maybe they're microscopic fish," Daniel offered.

I smiled down at him. "Could be they're on their fishy lunch break."

"I think they're just invisible." Daniel laughed, and just like always the sound made me relax a bit. Once his laughter fell away, the only sound was the low bubbling murmur of that aquarium filter. We stood there, quiet for a long time, I guess. Finally, still gazing into the empty water, my brother said, "Hey, Andi, how come you're mad at me?"

I knelt down and cupped his shoulders, wondering how long he'd been waiting to ask this particular question. "I'm not mad at you, Little Man. Nobody's mad at you."

He stared at the gray carpet. "Well then, how come you're mad at Mom?"

I winced. In the two days since the birth of the Abernathy baby, my mother and I had avoided each other altogether. Mostly she stayed in the main cabin and I did routine maintenance around the grounds, replacing a busted window in Cabin One, trimming back some rhododendrons trying to take over Cabin Three. Daniel had tuned in to the tension and kept to himself, rereading his comics and constructing a Lego spaceship from a kit my mother picked up for him at Cohler's. Finally, I made up a diplomatic answer. "We just don't always see things the same way."

Daniel rocked on his heels. He lifted his face so his brown eyes came into mine. "You guys are fighting about that baby girl."

It was always hard to hide things from Daniel, and even harder to lie outright to him. "Mom loves you and I love you. That's all you need to worry about." After a pause, I added, "Just remember, *you ain't special*, right?"

It'd been three years since I uttered this phrase, a kind of magical incantation I spoke with the same reverent tone I once reserved for solemn prayer, but Daniel seemed to recall it and nodded earnestly. *"I ain't special,"* he repeated, just like he used to. He looked a little sad.

You might think I'm a crappy sister for telling my kid brother that kind of thing, but before you judge me, you better hear about Mrs. Bundower. She was a sweet lady and the best seamstress in town, always the first choice for a wedding veil or a prom dress. (She made the one Michelle Kirkpatrick wore the night she deliberately drove her car off the cliff at McGinley's Cove.) When Mrs. Bundower's heart started going bad, everybody felt miserable. This was the summer after Daniel got rescued but before the fish died, so the people at the Universal Church of Paradise were still asking Daniel for favors with God. But even all those prayers didn't slow her steady decline, and finally she ended up at St. Jude's.

The night my mother said she wanted us all to visit, I didn't think too much of it, figuring Mrs. Bundower just wanted some company. At that point, I was convinced that she was going to recover. But when we walked into that dim room up on the fourth floor, Mrs. Bundower was still and gray, and I knew she wouldn't be getting better. Her eyes were open, but they were locked on the ceiling above her with no sign of recognition. Her head sat like a heavy stone, hard and deep in the pillow. The worst thing of all was how with every breath her jaw twitched as she sucked for air. It wasn't like the way a runner tries to catch her breath after a sprint. It was more like the way a fish washed on the rocks gasps — open-eyed, trying to fight off the inevitable.

Chief Bundower sat with his forehead pressed to the metal rail of the bed. I guess he'd seen enough of that face. He thanked my mother for coming, gave the latest report from the doctors. I remember the phrase, "Try to keep her comfortable." Sylvia Volpe stepped from the shadows behind the Chief to greet us. Daniel walked right over to Mrs. Bundower, just across from the Chief. He climbed up on a step stool, reached through the metal railing, and took one of her skeleton hands between his. I didn't like him touching her. The five of us prayed silently for a while, and I tried hard not to think of what Mrs. Bundower was or wasn't feeling. I hated the raspy wheezing of her breath and the look of her face, so, like the Chief, I just closed my eyes. That's why I didn't see Daniel till it was too late.

After a while, Mrs. Bundower stopped breathing, and that silence made me look up. Everybody focused on her and on the Chief's muffled sobbing. Volpe draped an arm over his shoulder, and my mother said, "I'm so sorry. I'll go get someone." She stepped into the hallway.

When I looked to see how Daniel was reacting, I couldn't believe what I saw. The flesh of his face was pale white and coated in a sweaty sheen. His hands were still locked around the dead woman's, and they were trembling, like he was trying to push something from his healthy body into her sick one. "Daniel," I said. "Let go."

His eyes popped open and he didn't seem to know who I was. I reached down and tried to pry his fingers free. "She's gone," I said.

"Gone to her just reward in heaven," Volpe corrected.

Daniel still didn't seem to understand what had happened. He kept blinking his eyes, like he was trying to wake up. Even after I got his hands free, he was still a zombie. I wiped the sweat from his forehead with a handkerchief and tried to get him to drink some water. Finally I shouted, "Little Man!" and he came around. He looked at Mrs. Bundower's corpse and tore out of the room.

It took me nearly fifteen minutes of jogging around the corridors, even checking the parking lot, but finally I noticed the cracked door of a broom closet just down the hallway. Daniel was huddled up on the floor in the dark, and he wasn't crying at all, but his body was shaking and his eyes were wide.

"I didn't pray good?" he asked me.

I settled down next to him. "You prayed great. Sometimes people just die."

"I didn't pray for her to die."

"God doesn't always do what we pray for." Now I had an arm around him.

"But I'm special in the eyes of the Lord. God smiles upon me."

He was only repeating what he'd been hearing up at the UCP

for weeks, but real fear took hold of my heart. What does it lead to, when a three-year-old thinks the world is defined by his desires? That good fortune is his to give, that death is a result of his failure? This had to stop. I took my brother's face in my hands, my palms pressed to his cheeks, and I aimed his eyes into mine. "Now you hear this. You ain't special. Got it? You're the same as everybody else. You ain't special."

"I ain't special." I could tell the idea comforted him some, though I don't doubt that he wondered if I was lying for his benefit. But I decided right then and there in that broom closet, that for his own good, I would stand against those trying to make my brother into some kind of junior miracle worker.

Of course, three years later, by the day we were back at St. Jude's to see the Abernathys' baby, a lot had happened. There were the fish and my dad, the ice storm. So I hadn't had to tell Daniel he wasn't special for quite some time. Hearing him repeat it to me in the visitors' room, looking into the empty aquarium, I realized I wasn't quite sure I fully believed it myself. I mean, I knew he couldn't do miracles, but Daniel did seem *different*. Without thinking it through, I asked him a question that'd been keeping me awake at night. "How'd you know the baby was going to be a girl?"

He shrugged his bony shoulders and wandered back to his comic book on the chair. "I dunno. I just thought it was gonna be a girl and it was."

I nodded. He did have a fifty-fifty chance, after all. "What made you sing like you did?"

His eyes roamed the space over my head and then he looked at me. "I thought Mrs. Abernathy would like it. Didn't she like it?"

"Sure she did, Little Man. It was nice what you did." I felt the weight of Daniel's anxious stare, so I added, "You did a great job. A super job."

But my reassurances weren't enough to make him smile. He chewed on a fingernail until I told him to quit.

"Hey, Andi," he said. "How come you didn't want me to go to Mrs. Abernathy's house?"

I knew I couldn't answer him, so I walked over to the picture window looking out across the parking lot. A red van slid into a handicapped spot. On the roof was a tiny satellite dish and on the side were letters I knew too well: WPBE. The Scranton television station, the same one that tried to rise to glory on my brother's rescue in the fairy fort, had broadcast a short piece the night before about the birth of the Abernathy baby. I hadn't seen it, but Gayle told me it was pretty lame. Now here they were, coincidentally at the very same time Daniel was in the building.

I turned and grabbed Daniel's hand to lead him toward the hallway. He dropped his comic and said, "What's wrong?"

"We got set up," I said. I wasn't sure if it was by Volpe or my mother or both. The hallway only had one exit, and the double set of elevators was down close to it. I worried we might run into the news crew, so I pulled Daniel toward the only good hiding place I could find: the ladies' room.

"Gross!" he said. "I ain't going in there."

I shoved him through the swinging door. "Get into a stall and stay put till I come for you. Do it."

No sooner had the bathroom door stilled than someone appeared in the hallway. But it was no newscaster. The middle-aged man emerged from the chapel, dressed in a black suit with a narrow tie, like he was going to church. He was thin as a scarecrow, and stubble dotted his sunken cheeks. His eyes, nervous and red, gave me the impression that he was terribly sick, and I wondered if he was in fact a patient. He didn't say anything at first, and when his roaming stare finally fell on me, he blinked like he was just coming awake.

"You that Miracle Boy's sister," he said, half a question and half a statement.

"No," I said. "You got me mixed up with somebody else."

Scarecrow scratched at his leg, clawing at his pants like he had an itch that wouldn't be satisfied. "I mark you for a liar, girl. Time was when I studied you and that boy up at the church by the lakeside."

It had been a long while since I'd been at the UCP. I searched my memory for this thin stranger's face. He kept talking. "I saw him again on the TV. Came here to see for myself the baby girl he helped birth. People around here are talking, saying that baby girl was dead and the boy brung her back to life. Like he claims to been brung back hisself."

"My brother never said that," I told him. "Other people made that up."

His face shifted and I realized I'd slipped something of the truth. He walked closer. "I wonder if your brother's a liar like you are."

My eyes fell to a fire alarm on the opposite wall. "My brother went upstairs," I said. "You got no business here."

He tilted his head and considered me. "My business is the Lord's business. I am His servant and I test for Him the wicked and the just. I ain't fixed yet on which your brother is, but the truth will come before me. If he is anointed by God, I have need of him."

I wasn't sure what that meant, but I knew I didn't like it. "He's just a little boy," I told him. "He's not special."

"A common charlatan?" he said. "A perpetrator of hoaxes? Then his charade must be exposed to the cleansing light."

I was ready to leap across the hall, yank that fire alarm, and hopefully flood the floor with evacuating patients and hospital personnel. But then the doors at the far end of the hallway split open, and a lady reporter with red hair and a bulky man with a camera started toward us. Scarecrow walked away, calm as you please, like we'd just chatted about the weather. I was going to yell, "Stop that guy," but I was scared myself, and just glad that he was gone.

Neither one of the WPBE folks recognized me. They looked inside the visitors' room and seemed puzzled. "Hey," I said, suddenly inspired. "You looking for the Miracle Boy?"

The redhead beamed a perfect TV smile and nodded. I said, "He's up on the third floor with the Abernathy baby. I heard the two of them were speaking in tongues."

The instant the elevator doors opened, they rushed in and disappeared. I was ready to be gone from that hospital. So I ducked into the ladies' room, found Daniel pinching his nose and holding one hand over his eyes, and dragged him out into the hallway. The doors to the second elevator were just closing, and my mother, Volpe, and Mr. Abernathy stood in the visitors' room doorway, looking around. They'd passed the news crew going up. Mr. Abernathy was holding the baby.

"Expecting somebody?" I said.

My mother seemed confused, but Volpe gave me a knowing look. Daniel strolled into the visitors' room and said, "How's that baby girl?" Mr. Abernathy bent down and tilted the bundle, angling the exposed face. When Daniel peeked inside, his eyes went wide with wonder.

Volpe circled me and got to the far side of Daniel. A camera with a long lens hung around her neck like an oversize piece of jewelry, and she lifted it and began snapping pictures. "The poor thing has been sleeping all day," she told us between shots. I just about snatched the camera from her hands, and I should have. Daniel called me over to see the baby, but I stayed where I was, arms crossed.

Mr. Abernathy rocked gently and smiled at my brother. "Say hello to Miracle Danielle Abernathy."

I thought *Miracle* sounded like a name for a racehorse, but I didn't say so. I turned to Mr. Abernathy and Volpe. "Listen, I don't know who's telling what kind of stories about Daniel, but you need to keep it to yourselves."

Without looking at me, Mr. Abernathy said, "Grace is simply sharing the truth with people. Why shouldn't she?"

"Well," I said, "your wife's version of reality isn't always the most reliable."

Everybody went dead quiet and instantly I wished I had the words back.

My mother sighed. "Oh, Ann."

"I'm sorry," I offered.

But Mr. Abernathy just shook his head. For the first time he faced me, looking across his shoulder. "I recognize that you've had some difficulties in your life. But that hardly gives you the right to be cruel."

I swallowed and looked at the busted TV. "I'm not trying to be cruel. I'm just trying to take care of my brother. Look, there was just some skinny nutjob in the hallway trying to find Daniel. He was spouting off about the UCP and testing Daniel, whatever the hell that means."

Daniel, clearly spooked, turned at this. I didn't say anything more for fear of really freaking him out.

"And where is this man now?" Volpe asked skeptically.

I looked at my mother to see if she believed me. She asked Daniel, "Did somebody scare you?"

"Andi made me hide in the ladies' bathroom."

You can imagine how this went over. I said, "I don't care if you believe me or not. It happened."

Everyone stared at each other for a few tense moments, then Daniel leaned in to the baby and said to me, "She's so tiny. Come see."

I stayed where I was.

Volpe snapped a few more shots with that camera. "Here now before you is the truest blessing of the Lord. Gaze upon this child and let your heart be lifted up."

My heart didn't feel especially heavy, and Mr. Abernathy didn't seem to care either way, but I really was feeling bad about what I'd said about his wife, so I stepped in closer as a kind of apology. Besides, even though I wouldn't have admitted it to anybody there that day, I wanted to see the baby for myself. Since the night of the birth, I'd had a hard time getting that scrunched-up face out of my mind, those sky blue eyes that stared right through me. So, not sure what to expect, I looked at Miracle.

Despite what you might have heard, she did not have golden

hair. There was no white glow surrounding her. No cross-shaped birthmark adorned her forehead. The fact is, her head was hairy and still shaped a little funny from being squeezed like it was. Her pink skin seemed flawless to me, not a scar or a freckle or a wrinkle to be found.

But if I'm going to be a full and true witness, I have to be honest and tell you something else. The air around Miracle was thick with that scent I couldn't quite place, the same one I smelled the night she was born. I was waiting for her to open her eyes, so I kept inhaling, sniffing at this scent you'd never expect from a baby or hospital. That baby girl smelled of vanilla, rich and pure, and there in that waiting room I remembered where I'd smelled it before: the fairy fort.

I almost asked if anyone else noticed it, but I was afraid they might think I was making some kind of joke.

"She's great, Mr. Abernathy," I said. "I'm glad she's okay and hope Mrs. Abernathy's okay."

He nodded at me but said nothing. Volpe piped up, "Grace's placenta ruptured, but she's recovering nicely. Dr. Ghadari expects to release her in the morning. She's resting now, but when she wakes, I'll tell her that you send your good wishes and prayers."

I didn't like Volpe putting words in my mouth, let alone prayers. I was on the verge of correcting her, but Daniel said, "Baby Miracle's having a little dream."

We all leaned in and looked closely, but the sleeping child's face seemed no different to me.

Volpe asked, "What is she dreaming about?"

Daniel glanced at my mother and then at me, as if seeking permission. Neither of us told him not to answer, so he did.

"About angels. All babies come from heaven but they forget when they start growing up. So she's dreaming all about it while she still remembers."

This delighted Volpe, who got so choked up she had to tug a white handkerchief from her pocket. "God's greatest blessing," she said, fighting back tears as she poked a folded corner up inside her gold glasses.

When her cell phone rang, it startled us all. She answered it and listened, then said, "No, we're downstairs. Yes, in the visitors' room."

"Time for us to go, Ma," I said.

Volpe shot me a sharp look.

"What's this about?" my mother said.

"It's about us leaving," I told her. I took Daniel's hand and started for the door, but something anchored me.

Volpe had ahold of his other hand. She bent down and said, "I never stopped believing in you, Daniel. Lo these many trials, I never once doubted." Her eyes were bright and shiny, the way eyes get just before tears come on. "I swear by the grace of God," she said, "others will know what you've done here. I will spread word of the wonders you have worked."

Over my dead body, you psycho bitch, I thought.

And that's as good a place as any to mark as the birth of the Anti-Miracle Plan.

CHAPTER THREE

There was a time when the whole world prayed for Daniel. Maybe you were part of it. Maybe, like tens of thousands of true believers, you closed your eyes and pressed your palms tight together and begged whatever God rules your heaven to please help that poor boy who'd been swallowed up by the earth. I did. That second night in the woods east of Roosevelt Park, I prayed as hard as anybody ever prayed in the history of praying. And for a while, it seemed to work.

When Daniel first disappeared in the forest, I assumed he was messing around, being a pain like little brothers can be. Just three years old, he'd tagged along with Jeff Cedars and me on a hike up to the fairy fort, a collection of ancient stones stacked in towers and circular patterns. Irene McGinley and the other Irish immigrants were the first to call it a fairy fort, but legend has it that even the Indians who lived in the valley way back when didn't know who'd set up the stones or why. They dealt with the mystery by showing the stones respect and leaving them alone — wisdom I wish I had followed.

The fairy fort is up above the wild apple orchard in this giant depression in the ground, like a huge sinkhole or a prehistoric crater, big as a football field. No trees grow in the fort, but leaves and pine needles drift down every fall, and when Jeff and I realized

Daniel wasn't in sight, we charged around the stones, kicking through the thick carpet, hollering out Daniel's name. There was no way he could've climbed out of the fort without us seeing, so he had to be playing hide-and-seek. But after ten minutes, I started getting pretty ticked off. My mother would be putting dinner on soon enough, and Dad would be crazy mad if we were late.

Twenty minutes after Daniel disappeared, a light drizzle began to pitter-patter the leaves and darken the stones. Jeff said, "Something's not right. What if he's not playing around?"

"Get my dad," I told him. "I'll stay here and keep looking."

When Jeff returned, he had not only my dad with him, but Chief Bundower too, being tugged ahead by Pinkerton. The old bloodhound strained against the end of the leash, sliding his head back and forth as he sniffed at the ground. The Chief held one of Daniel's shirts in his other hand. Pinkerton weaved through the stones, settled for an instant here, then there, and finally stopped to paw like crazy at some wet leaves. We were confused at first because it seemed like he was digging at solid earth. Then the Chief bent over and said to my dad, "Charles, there's something here."

The Chief dropped onto all fours, pushed the dog away, and began yelling Daniel's name down into the ground. When I got close, I saw the hole, a ragged mouth the size of a small bucket, hardly large enough for a horseshoe. My dad scratched an eyebrow. "Danny couldn't fit through there, Earl. All your damn dog found us was a rabbit hole."

But the Chief had faith in Pinkerton. He stood up, snapped the walkie-talkie from his belt, and radioed the state police. When he signed off and replaced the walkie-talkie, he put one hand on my father's shoulder. "Charles, PT's never been wrong. Your boy is in that hole and we've got to get him out."

That was around eight or nine o'clock at night. Over the next few hours, emergency rescue teams began showing up — from Hawley, from Wilkes-Barre, from Hazleton. They brought hard hats and shovels and gas-powered generators. One of them pitched a blue tarp over the hole to keep out the rainwater. Near as they could tell, the hole went down at least twenty feet, probably more. Somebody decided it was probably an ancient well and nobody questioned him. Other than Pinkerton's nose, we had no reliable proof that Daniel was down there. A group of firefighters wanted to widen the hole, but some miner from Scranton said the only chance was to dig a parallel shaft and tunnel over. Problem with that was they'd be estimating where Daniel was and they'd need to haul drilling equipment up into the forest.

I heard all of this from a position I'd taken atop a fist-shaped gray rock overlooking the hole. I just sat there in the light rain, watching everything like you do in a dream. Part of me thought maybe Daniel was off someplace hiding, upset that Jeff and I didn't pay him enough attention or something. That's what I was hoping. But in my gut, I knew my brother was down there trapped.

Somewhere in the middle of the night, the rain stopped and the chain saws started. Every available man, Jeff and my dad included, had been recruited to clear-cut a ten-foot-wide path between the fairy fort and the field so the drilling equipment could get through. That's nearly a quarter mile, and they worked from both ends. When I tried to help, my dad told me to go down to the picnic pavilions, where the women were holding a prayer vigil. Instead I crept back to the hole and talked to Daniel. I told him not to worry, that everything would be okay. When I ran out of things to say, I thought about how tired I was and how tired he must be, so I sang him some lullabies. And when I ran out of lullabies, I sang whatever I could think of, songs about John Jacob Jingleheimer Schmidt and Rudolph the Red-nosed Reindeer.

I don't think I fell asleep during those hours. I remember the constant growl of chain saws growing dimmer as they made progress away from the fort, and I remember the stars overhead fading as the sky began to turn from black to dark blue. Then a mechanical roar buzzed the tops of the pines and a great cone of light swung over us. I stood and saw the helicopter, floating west toward the park. As I charged down the new trail, past the carnage of jagged stumps and felled trees, my mind filled with a vision of experts, trained professionals from New York or Philadelphia, people who planned for disasters like this every day. They'd have a better idea than this half-baked drilling plan, and they'd have Daniel free in no time. When I reached the forest's edge, I saw the helicopter, already landed just beyond FDR's statue. In its lights, two men climbed out, one oddly wearing a sports jacket. The other reached back into the belly of the helicopter and pulled out gear that at first I thought might save my brother. But then the man heaved it up onto his shoulder and I recognized it for what it was: a camera. On the tail of the helicopter I found the letters WPBE.

I had no way of knowing that they'd beam our story out in time for the morning news on regional affiliates, or that the national networks would pick it up by midday. They filmed the crews of would-be lumberjacks hacking away at the pine trees and took long shots of the silent hole. Mrs. Wheeler slipped an arm over my mother's shoulder and convinced her to talk to the press. The cameras zoomed in on their crying faces, and that's when my mother and Mrs. Wheeler asked for all those watching to pray for Daniel. Much of America woke up to that story — a small town in Pennsylvania was desperately trying to save a boy who had fallen into the earth. And that boy needed your prayers.

By lunchtime the men finished dragging the amputated pines off to the side of the new path, and the drilling equipment got hauled up slowly over the fresh stumps. Three more news crews had arrived by then, and together they reduced what seemed like the greatest tragedy to ever strike our town to witty phrases like "Peril in Paradise." It took most of the afternoon to drill the rescue tunnel, but the lead story on the evening news was going to be one of hope. Soon rescuers would finish the tunnel. Young Daniel would be in his mother's arms before nightfall. Americans from coast to coast, and viewers across the world, held their breath.

I was on my perch atop that gray rock when the rescue tunnel collapsed. They had extracted the drill, and that miner from Scranton had been strapped into a harness, which was attached to a winch set up over the opening. The hard hat he wore had a light on its forehead. He held a shovel that seemed like a kid's toy. But from what I could hear, they thought the rescue tunnel was only a few feet away from Daniel, and the miner would carefully dig sideways until he reached my brother. That was the plan. But just a few minutes after they lowered him down the rescue hole, the earth sighed and the ground between the two holes sagged.

I didn't understand at first why everyone began shouting,

why those manning the winch began yelling, "Get him up! Get him up!" When the miner emerged, his face was black with dirt, and he coughed and gasped for breath. A paramedic bent over him.

The men around Daniel's hole were on their knees, and one of them began to cry. The miner's efforts had caused the hole to cave in. My three-year-old brother was now buried alive.

I can't even begin to tell you how I felt, partly because I don't want to think about it.

But this was now the grim news that beamed out in time for the six o'clock broadcasts. If you see snippets of those old programs now, you can tell that people had given up. There was more talk of a recovery team than rescue efforts. The local news crew left, maybe out of respect, maybe because somebody didn't think a limp body being pulled from the earth would make good television. But the other crews stayed, and they kept filming while the men deliberated and decided to drill another tunnel.

That second night was harder. Listening to the whirling whine of the drilling machine, I tried to believe my brother could still be alive somehow. I tried to pray. I tried not to be angry at God, but it was hard. I mean, if everything happened according to God's plan, then God intended for Daniel to fall down that well. He intended for my brother — a child completely without sin — to be cold and wet and terrified, or dead. And He meant for me to feel this crushing guilt.

Still, I thought it was important to try and pray, and after a while I just started saying, "Please God, let Daniel live." I repeated it over and over, for hours really, and I rocked with a rhythm like when I ran, until finally my body surrendered to exhaustion.

I woke up when the drilling machine shut off, and I was worried about what the silence meant. The second rescue tunnel had taken twice as long to finish, but it was done. I crawled down off my rock and pushed through the small crowd to see the giant tripod they'd set up over the new opening. The winch at the top looked like an oversize reel from a fishing rod. A second miner appeared, dressed just like the first: a harness of thick black straps and a hard hat with a light on it. Someone snapped the metal line from the reel onto the harness, and just as the sun sliced through the pines, he was lowered into the second tunnel. This was going out live on all the television networks that had cameras there. The same viewers who'd woken up the day before to the first news of the disaster were now watching to see the outcome.

The second rescue tunnel was farther away from Daniel's tunnel than the first, so that miner had quite a way to dig sideways. Because everyone was straining to hear the miner on his walkie-talkie, somebody cut off the power generators and the fairy fort filled with an eerie silence. But then all of us gathered around the hole turned to a strange sound — a soft chanting rising up from the meadow. Down in the open field, my mother and Mrs. Wheeler and the Cullen sisters and Mr. Hogan and the Abernathys and maybe two dozen others had fallen to their knees and joined hands in a prayer circle. In the early morning mist coming off the lake, they sang hymns in hopes of persuading God to resurrect my baby brother. It's all on the video.

On the other side of the hole, my father shook his head.

Twenty anxious minutes later, the miner radioed up, but the crackling static couldn't be understood. And then the winch was reeling slowly backward and I realized they were drawing him out. I expected he was coming out to take a break or get other equipment. His hard hat appeared and then his whole body, dangling in the air.

His back was turned to me at first, so I didn't see him clutching Daniel. But over the weeks and months to come, I saw that snippet of film so many times that now it's part of my memory of the actual event. These are the images I share with the world: Daniel's blackened face. The harsh scrape on his bloodied cheek. His head strapped to the board for his own safety. And his dark brown eyes, blinking and wet, but proof positive that he was alive.

Everyone cheered and screamed and wept with joy. Even the big men. They all cried like babies.

I'll bet you saw all this, but you never saw me, did you? That's 'cause I stayed off to the side, out of the camera's view. I leaned into the fist-shaped rock and bowed my head. I imagined God watching over us all and I thanked Him. Daniel had been saved and my prayer had been answered. Despite all the troubling thoughts I'd had during the long night, when my brother emerged unharmed from that hole in the morning brightness, I felt certain that God was really looking out for us after all.

The wind picked up and the pine trees above the fairy fort shivered, and the breeze brought that smell to me: vanilla. It was the same thing I would smell when Miracle was born, and later too. And to this very day, I'm not completely sure what to make of it.

CHAPTER FOUR

The morning after I had my run-in with the Scarecrow and Volpe up at St. Jude's, my mother drove Daniel over to the Abernathys' with a bowl of potato casserole to welcome the family home. When I told her my plans to head in to the *Gazetteer*, she said she could drop me off, even though it was out of her way. I told her I'd be fine on my own and walked into town alone. In the office, I locked the door behind me and kept the blinds down. Gayle typically didn't show up till around lunchtime, so I knew I'd have the only computer to myself for a few hours while I worked on a special project.

The Scarecrow's talk of healers and charlatans inspired me, and online I tracked down a half dozen "miracle workers" who'd been exposed as fakes. There was a woman from Kansas with bleeding palms, an Iowa farmer struck six times by lightning, a preacher who claimed his kiss could heal. That last guy gets the gold medal for being both a fraud and, quite clearly, a class AAA pervert. I cranked out a rough draft of an article summarizing their experiences, focusing on how each one was eventually exposed as a quack. The stigmata woman was charging a hundred dollars per "consultation" until somebody caught her taking a razor to her hands, and it turns out that preacher had seven wives in as many states. I wanted to show the *Gazetteer* readers the facts behind the hysteria that surrounds a supposed miracle worker.

Of course, everybody in town knew I had some experience as a debunker of miraculous acts. My infamous senior-year journalism project at Paradise High School was an exposé of the plagues that supposedly convinced the pharaoh to let Moses and the Israelites leave Egypt. The frogs, the locusts, the water turned to blood. But I located all kinds of scientific studies that suggested that these were in fact naturally occurring phenomena, many linked directly to the eruption of the Santorini Volcano in the Aegean Sea. Once its ash infected the Nile, the water changed color and the fish died from lack of oxygen. Their rotting corpses drove the frogs up onto land and brought the horde of flies, which carried disease that killed the youngest children, since their immune systems were the least developed. It was a chain reaction of crazy coincidences. Taken as a whole, it seemed like divine intervention. This was exactly what had happened when Daniel got pulled out of the well, but now that chain reaction was starting again, and I had to stop it before it got out of hand.

Why, I kept wondering, did all these people believe in the first place — in Daniel's power or Irene McGinley's curse or a Kansas woman with bleeding palms? It was one thing in the time of Moses, sure, but these days, with cell phones and satellite dishes, I couldn't understand why the world clung to such superstitious crap.

I was just printing up a revision of my article when Gayle came in through the back door of the *Gazetteer* office holding two bags from Victorio's.

"Got you the special," she said, depositing one white bag on the desk next to me. "Meatball sandwich and a bag of chips." This struck me as odd, since I usually didn't come in on Saturdays, and I expected Gayle to be surprised I was there. But she just shuffled to the big table by the front window and opened the shades. "You going vampire on me or something?" she asked. She got started on her own lunch, a salad piled high with tomatoes. Gayle's weight was something she'd been struggling with since I met her. She'd tried pills, patches, hypnosis, even adopted a stray dog to get her to walk every morning, but she couldn't lose a pound. Every day I worked at the *Gazetteer*, she bought me lunch. She never once asked me what I wanted, and over time I realized she was buying me the food she really felt like eating.

I unraveled the aluminum foil and took a few bites from my sandwich, trying to work up the courage to show Gayle my article. The first sentence read, "Human history has been a forward progression from ignorance to illumination." Ever since I had done a high school internship with Gayle, she and I got along pretty well, but she wasn't one for favors when it came to using the paper for personal reasons.

She took a swig of her flavored bottled water. "Saw Jeff Cedars driving with his mom up by the Carlsons' this morning."

I didn't make any response. Of course with all that was going on, I'd thought about Jeff plenty, but he had his life and I had mine.

"Wasn't he taking summer session?"

I shrugged, kept my eyes on the computer screen. "Maybe it's over."

"So you haven't talked to him?"

"No, Gayle. I haven't." Now I tried to give her the hard look that meant *drop the subject.*

Even though Jeff's a couple years older than me, we hung out all through middle school, just friends who liked to hike the trails deep into the woods or paddle around the lake on the metal canoes his dad rented out, before he upgraded to Jet Skis during the big boom. In high school, when Jeff started wrestling and I started track, we ran together every day before class. I found myself passing the day by marking when I'd see him again. Over time, our feelings grew beyond a simple word like *friendship,* though we never talked about dating or used goofy terms like *girlfriend* or *boyfriend.* Halfway through my freshman year, we started holding hands on those mountain walks, and our morning jogs were sometimes interrupted.

Those days, Jeff would be the first person I talked to about any problems. But after Daniel's rescue, we'd drifted apart. In all the excitement, with Daniel in the hospital, with all those folks with the cameras in our driveway, it wasn't hard to find excuses for not getting together. When he was leaving for college and came to say good-bye, we hugged but didn't kiss. Not even on the cheek. His first year at Penn State, he sent me a couple letters about his classes and life in the dorms, and we ran into each other at a New Year's party. That summer, he might wave if he drove by our dock on a Jet Ski, and I might wave back. After his sophomore year, he stayed at Penn State for the summer, so I was surprised to hear he was coming back home this June. I wondered now if he'd heard about the Abernathy baby. I wondered if he thought about Daniel or about me.

Gayle pushed her salad around with the plastic fork. "I'll bet you some sorority gal has got ahold of him."

Clearly my eye contact wasn't backing her off the topic. "Free country," I said. I turned back to my article. A moment later, something whacked into the side of my head. The plastic lid of Gayle's salad container wobbled like a Frisbee on the ground next to me.

"Hey," she said. "Truce. I didn't mean any harm by my poking. I just always figured you two might have some kind of reunion. You were sweet together."

"Well," I said. "The past is the past."

Gayle nodded her head to show she agreed, then changed subjects. "How's the meatball?"

"Not enough sauce," I told her.

She started talking about some of the work we had to get done, mostly layout on ads, a couple obits, and polishing silly articles like "Ten New Uses for Your Old Socks." Truth be told, Gayle didn't need me all that much. Once my internship was officially over, I just kept hanging around. I'd deferred my track scholarship to Lock Haven for a year so I could stick close and keep an eye on Daniel, and I had no luck finding other work in a dying town like Paradise. Every now and then Gayle would give me an envelope with a few twenties in it. I guess she realized I wasn't listening to her agenda for the afternoon, because finally she just said, "Hey, where's your head?"

I shifted in the chair, put down my sandwich, and said, "How many years of law school did you finish?"

"Two years of pre-law," she said. "How come?"

"What do you know about restraining orders?"

She pulled her chair over to mine and set her salad on her lap. "You better tell me what this is about."

I gave Gayle the short version of my encounter with the Scarecrow, and from the look on her face, I could tell she believed me more than my mother did. Not that that was hard. She lifted her chin and rubbed at her jowly neck. "I can't see how a judge could issue a restraining order against a stranger. You don't even know this guy's name. On top of all that, the last place you saw him was forty-five miles away."

What she said made sense, but it was good just to have someone else share my concern. "He talked about the UCP like he's been there," I said. "I've got to do something."

"Maybe go talk to Bundower," she offered. "Be on the safe side."

I'd thought about the Chief myself but figured that he, like my mother, would just blow me off. "The problem is bigger than just this one guy," I said. I picked up the article I'd spent all morning on and handed it to her.

Gayle wiped a napkin across her mouth. "What you got?"

I watched her eyes scan back and forth across the lines, narrow and tight as if she was thinking hard. Before she got through the opening paragraphs, though, her head was already shaking side to side. "This won't do you a damn bit of good."

"What do you mean?"

"You're trying to reason folks out of a position that's got nothing to do with reason. These things are matters of faith. People believe with their hearts, Anderson, not their heads. All this story will do is make you seem pissy. Nobody'll change their mind."

I knew instantly that what she was saying was right, but I didn't want to admit it. "Print it and let's find out."

She handed the story back to me. "Nah. Can't do that. Won't do it. Besides the fact that it's a dumbass idea you're too thick-headed to see, the whole town knows you work here, and publishing this would make us seem biased. Journalists are supposed to stay objective."

"Don't lecture me, Gayle. This ain't the *New York Times*."

She put the story down and aimed that white fork up at me, stared at me along it like a rifle. "No, it's the *Five Mountains Gazetteer*, and it's my paper. When you're the publisher and editor, you can decide what goes into it."

I looked away from her, out the window at Roosevelt Road. A school bus painted white rumbled by, with a blue cross and words I couldn't read scrawled along the side like graffiti. A bus like that had no place in our town, none that would make me happy at least. I scratched at my forehead.

Gayle said, "Listen, since you're already all riled up, may as well tell you that we'll be running a story on the baby."

"The baby," I repeated. "Miracle?"

"It's news, Anderson. And that's our business, remember? Even with Paradise Days just around the corner, all anybody's talking about is that baby girl and Daniel. You should hear what they're saying over at Vic's. Cooper Reynolds swears his migraines are gone. Scotty Mitchell's stutter has cleared up. And Sally Guth is late."

"Late for what?"

"Her period. She and Jim have been trying for two years to conceive."

I could feel my jaw sticking out. "And somehow Daniel is responsible for this? How? You know it's all just coincidence. C'mon, Gayle, you can't believe any of this miracle bullshit."

"What I believe doesn't matter. But a lot of the people who buy papers see these things as signs and wonders. I have an obligation."

"Guess I just didn't realize how many of your subscribers were royal nutjobs."

She spiked her fork into the salad and huffed. "Don't be like this. You know how things are. Besides, Sylvia's got some cute shots of that baby, and I already talked to your mom."

Now those two bags from Victorio's made sense. She'd been to the Abernathys' and found out I was coming here. I said, "So you already interviewed my mother for that story?"

Defiant, Gayle nodded her head. "We talked."

"And you're going to run one of Volpe's pictures of Daniel and that baby?"

"It's a human interest story. I'm in the business of selling papers."

"Unbelievable. This'll only make everything worse. You don't even care about my side of the story."

"I know your side of it, Anderson. Everybody south of Scranton knows your side of it. Don't you get it? Nobody wants to hear it. These people want to believe."

"Volpe and the crazies do," I said. Before I really knew what I was doing, I was walking toward the front door. When I snapped it open, the little bell chimed stupidly on top.

Gayle shoved her chair back and followed me out onto the sidewalk. "Come back in here and finish your lunch. We got work to do."

I looked up and down the street, wondering about the crazy beat-up bus, but it was gone. "No," I told Gayle. "I think maybe I'll take a few sick days. I need time to sort this thing out."

People across the road were looking now, and those walking past ducked their heads like they weren't listening. I knew word would spread quickly that Anderson Grant had had another one of her hysterical fits, but I didn't care.

Gayle stepped over close to me, took my arm in her hand, and said quietly, "You're always jumping into things without thinking them through. Be careful, Andi. I don't want you getting hurt."

Looking back, Gayle was damn near a prophet, but I didn't heed her warning. Instead I started the long walk home, knowing that I'd probably just lost a valuable ally. If I was going to save Daniel, I couldn't do it alone.

Hiding behind a thick pine tree, resting my face into the hard bark, I watched Jeff Cedars for almost half an hour. He was cleaning off his father's Jet Skis one by one, sitting on each seat as the tiny crafts bobbed on the surface of the lake, scrubbing their colorful bodies with a soapy yellow sponge that he dunked now and then into a blue bucket above him on the dock. The Jet Skis were dirty from just sitting around in storage, but with Paradise Days nearing, Mr. Cedars needed them to be ready for rental. I decided that this must have been what brought Jeff home from college — his parents' call to come help.

Even though it didn't really matter, Jeff cleaned each Jet Ski until it shined, taking pride in his work. Every so often, he'd climb up to the dock and blast the suds with a hose. The sun was warm, and while I watched, Jeff slid his T-shirt over his buzzed head. In high school, Jeff was always on these crazy diets to make weight for wrestling. But he worked out and stayed in good shape, and it looked like his three years at college had added more than a few pounds of muscle. Tight squares on his abdomen suggested a regimen of sit-ups. The patch of hair that had once been just a ragged little triangle in the middle of his chest had spread out to the size of a hand. I could remember when his chest was perfectly smooth, and I wondered what it might feel like to run my fingers through that soft diamond.

I wasn't really sure how I'd come to be behind that tree. I guess I have to give credit, or maybe blame, to my legs. It's ironic as hell now, but all through middle and high school, my legs were the only part of me that I really liked. An ugly bump rose up on the bridge of my nose from when I busted it diving into a submerged rock. My chest was (still is) flat. My arms were too skinny, and my feet were too big. But my legs — they were slender and lean, tight and hard with muscles I'd earned. I'm not one of these girls obsessed with her looks, and I never really cared what anybody else thought of my legs. But they'd helped me win a lot of races and hadn't let me down when I needed them most, so I came to trust their instincts. When they said move, I moved.

As I had walked away from Gayle's, I got to making a kind of inventory of all the citizens of Paradise, trying to think of which ones were less crazy than others and which ones might help me and which ones might have some idea of how to stop the miracle machine. The idea to try to find my dad passed through my head, but I pushed that out. The rest of my list was pretty short. All the while, though, my legs were leading me to Jeff, a fact I didn't realize until I nearly stepped into the clearing that looks down on his family's dock. But I heard the hose and caught myself — like waking up from a dream — just in time to slip behind that pine. If it were up to my legs, I'd have marched right out into the open, I'm sure.

But now Jeff had wiped down the last of the Jet Skis and was climbing up onto the dock. He carried the bucket into the boathouse and when he came out, his T-shirt was on and he was making a beeline for his father's white van. I imagined him driving that van back to school, leaving me here alone again. And with that, my legs moved me out from behind the tree. "Yo, Cedars," I heard myself say.

Jeff turned and found my eyes immediately, and when he did, he smiled. "Yo, Grant." He stood where was he was, shoved his hands into the pockets of his shorts. "You interested in renting a really freaking clean Jet Ski?"

I skirted the water, stepping from rock to rock, then jumped up on the dock before he had a chance to offer his hand. "Nah. Those things don't have enough speed for me."

He grinned. Face-to-face, we had that awkward moment where we couldn't decide if we should hug or not. Since Jeff's a little shorter than me, he looked up to try and read my eyes to see what I'd want. We leaned together then leaned back, as if some magnetic force repelled our bodies. Maybe it was guilt. After a few seconds, he held up one hand and dangled car keys. "I'm sorry, but my dad's been down at Al's getting his hair cut. My mom asked me to go pick him up. You feel like a ride?"

I couldn't tell if he wanted me to come along or not, but I couldn't let him go. I shrugged my shoulders and said, "Got nothing else to do."

We climbed into the van and cranked the big doors shut. A Christmas tree air freshener hung from the rearview mirror, but I didn't smell anything. It could've been the same one that had hung there for years. I also recognized the duct tape that patched the seat.

"So how's your dad doing?" I asked, just trying to be polite.

"It's a day-by-day thing," Jeff said. "My mom said he's really trying."

"That's great," I said.

Jeff started the car and pulled out. Just that spring, Chief Bundower had picked up Jeff's father, drunk and asleep behind the wheel, two blocks from the Dog Bar Cantina. Word around town was that the Chief had overlooked two previous incidents, including one that ended with Mr. Cedars' van in a ditch. So after his third strike, Jeff's dad puttered around town on a red bicycle with a basket on the front or had Mrs. Cedars drive him wherever he needed to go. I didn't want to tell Jeff, but a couple times, I'd seen that red bike outside the Dog Bar.

As we headed north on Roosevelt Road, I started squirming with the silence. I asked, "So how'd your classes end up this semester?"

"Not too bad," Jeff said. "Got A's in Sociology of the Family and Environmental Science. Got a B in Applications in Critical Thinking, and a C in History of Landscape Architecture."

"Landscape Architecture?"

"Yeah, it's like designing parks and stuff like that."

Even though the road twists and curves like crazy, Jeff rested his palms loosely on the steering wheel. I saw that his fingernails were trimmed neat and tight. All during high school, he'd had a bad habit of biting at them when he was nervous.

Jeff honked twice and waved as we neared three backpackers walking on the side of the road. I guess he was assuming he knew them. But as we passed, they turned their heads and we saw they were strangers. I wondered why they were in Paradise, on foot.

"So what happened to all your hair?" I asked. "You lose a bet or something?"

He ran a hand over his crew cut. "Coach talked a few of us into an off-season tournament in May. We buzzed our heads to show solidarity, or something like that. It's comfortable for the summer, but come fall I'm going to let it grow out again."

"You should keep it," I said. "It looks nice." Then I wished I hadn't said something that might sound like a come-on. It was just strange, because Jeff had always been funny about his hair, keeping it long to cover a cauliflower ear he got from all those beatings on the wrestling mat. Now there it was, bumpy and exposed for all the world to see.

"Still running?" he asked.

"About every day," I answered. "Penn State's got a good gym, I guess."

He smirked. "About six. And they're crazy nice. Even the crappiest one is better than Paradise High's workout room. It's funny, though. I snuck in with the football team the other morning, and it was good to get back to those beat-up free weights. Maybe we just like things that are familiar, you know?"

"Maybe so," I said distractedly. Other than track, high school wasn't something I missed a whole lot.

"You still heading for Lock Haven come August?"

"That's the plan," I said, but it came out without energy or enthusiasm. I rolled my window down and let the air push against my face. It was good to see Jeff, but our conversation felt forced and awkward. It seemed like both of us were searching for questions just to keep the silence from filling the van.

What I wanted was to tell Jeff I was doing great, that my decision to defer my track scholarship for a year had been the absolute right one, no questions asked. I wanted to say that now I felt like Daniel was safe and when the fall rolled around I could leave for Lock Haven and get on with a life of my own. All this, of course, would have been a lie. "Jeff," I said without thinking, "I need to talk."

Jeff nodded and turned into the dirt parking lot of Amazing Animals, a roadside zoo that housed a dozen lame exhibits — an obese porcupine, anxious prairie dogs, a stuffed bison with a missing horn. After fallen pine trees smashed through a retaining wall during the ice storm, Samson the blind bear and a puma had escaped. The puma got hit by a snowplow over on Highway 71, but Samson disappeared forever in that ice storm, like my father. Now and then you'd hear a story about somebody spotting the bear, but he had surely died of starvation long ago.

"Keep driving," I said. "You shouldn't keep your dad waiting."

Jeff shut off the engine. "I heard about Daniel," he said, staring straight through the windshield. "I should've called you."

"Well," I said. "It's a weird deal."

"I didn't know if you'd want me to call."

I understood how he felt, but didn't know what to say back. "So what did you hear?"

"For starters, that Daniel walked across the lake last Saturday night when the Abernathys called."

"You got to be shitting me."

"Nope," Jeff said. "I also heard that Mrs. Abernathy's baby was born dead. Daniel prayed and brought it back to life."

I thought of Daniel's song and the smell of vanilla. I felt strangely conflicted but didn't want Jeff to know, so I asked, "Did you hear about Scotty Mitchell?"

Jeff nodded. "He lost his stutter. Anybody tell you about Mrs. Richardson's hemorrhoids?"

I held my hands up to stop him. "This town is so freaking lame. Even its miracles suck."

Jeff laughed. Then he asked, "So how's Little Man doing?"

"He's great," I said. "Always great."

Jeff smiled at the thought of Daniel, and I realized I was smiling too. I remembered the times the three of us went off together, for trips around the lake in one of Mr. Cedars' canoes or on afternoon hikes in the mountains. How easy it used to be for me to pretend we were a family of sorts. Of course, one of those long walks is what got us all into trouble in the first place.

"It'll blow over," Jeff assured me. "Just like last time."

"I'm not taking that chance."

"Chance of what? Come on, we're talking about hemorrhoids and stuttering. The town's just looking for a little excitement to spice up the summer."

I took a breath and, same as I told Gayle, I gave Jeff the story about Scarecrow. He listened closely, and when I finished, he shook his head. "Guy sounds certifiably nuts. You think he might show up at the church, cause trouble?"

"I'm not real interested in finding out," I said. "But it isn't just him. I saw Volpe's eyes. I saw Mr. Abernathy. And I remember last time. What if it gets worse, Jeff? What if people keep coming this time, keep wanting Daniel to be a miracle worker?"

Jeff shrugged. "They'll be disappointed?"

"It could get ugly," I corrected him. I wondered again about those three backpackers, and the white school bus. "Sometimes, not all the time, when he gets praying real hard, something happens to Daniel."

"Something like what?"

"He gets sick or something. Starts running a fever, gets all sweaty. A couple times, like when he was praying for Mrs. Bundower, it looked like he was going to die. Some of those nutjobs thought he could bring the fish back to life! We got lucky last time around, plain and simple. Daniel didn't get hurt or too screwed up. I'm not risking that again."

Now Jeff looked worried. "I don't see a whole lot you can do about what other people believe."

"I could take him," I said quietly, looking down Roosevelt Road. "I could run."

Jeff's hand rose up to his mouth and he ran his front teeth over a nail, but he didn't bite. A delivery truck pulled in behind us and a guy got out, walked up to the gates of Amazing Animals and cupped his eyes to the window. Jeff honked and yelled, "They ain't open on Saturdays till noon." The guy stared at Jeff like he thought this was stupid, then walked back to his truck and pulled out a cell phone. Jeff watched him for a minute before turning back to me. "You're going to kidnap Daniel?"

I shook my head. "It's only kidnapping if you demand a ransom, technically speaking. I looked it up online."

"Technically speaking? Oh, hell then, it's a fine idea. I'm sure your mom wouldn't have the freaking state police on your ass in like two seconds flat. Where would you go? How would you get there?"

This was something that had crossed my mind. *Maybe Penn State*, I wanted to say. *Maybe we could hide with you.*

But Jeff didn't offer sanctuary. "Running's in your blood, everybody knows that. But this, this'd just be crazy."

I knew he was right. My escape plan was the worst kind of fantasy. I decided then to ask him what I hadn't dared to ask Gayle. "You think I could convince a judge that my mother is endangering Daniel's health?"

"What could a judge do?"

"Give me custody."

"Legal custody of your brother? That makes sense. After all, your mom only feeds him dog food and makes him live in that ratty cardboard box. You've had crazier ideas, but I can't think of one right now."

I'd figured the same thing, but I guess I had to have somebody else say it.

Jeff asked, "Any chance your dad might help?"

Looking out my window, I pictured his Jeep driving off in the snow. I said, "No chance."

"But are you sure he even knows —"

"Drop it."

"Just asking. I didn't realize it was bite-Jeff's-head-off day."

"I don't mean to be pissy," I said. "I just don't know what to do."

We fell quiet again. That delivery guy drove off in his truck.

"Okay," Jeff said. "The first step in productive solutions is framing the nature of the problem."

I gave Jeff a look. "Where'd you hear that crap?"

"Professor Mullins. Applications in Critical Thinking."

"The class you got a B in?"

"Seriously, tell me as clearly as you can exactly what you want."

I decided to play along. "I want everybody to leave Daniel alone. Forever."

"All right. Now, what actions could affect that change?"

I thought about this, then held up my empty hands. "If the whole world forgot about the rescue and all the stuff afterward?"

"I'm not sure we can enforce global amnesia. That solution is non-workable."

"Right," I said.

"But what if something happened to make the people who believe in Daniel think maybe they were wrong? That they've been wrong all along?"

"That'd be kick-ass. But I think your solution is non-workable too."

"Seriously. We could say it was all a hoax in the first place — isn't that what the Scarecrow dude said?"

"Now we're taking our plans from nutjobs?"

"I'm just throwing out ideas," Jeff said. "It's called brainstorming."

"It's called a waste of time," I said. I looked at the watch on Jeff's wrist. "Your dad has got to be wondering what's keeping you. If he calls your mom, she'll be worried."

Jeff stared at me, then started the ignition and pulled back onto Roosevelt Road. A few silent minutes later, we reached the driveway that winds down to Camp Anderson and he pulled over to the side. "I didn't mean to get you all ticked off."

"I was upset when I came to find you."

"Severe emotional states are not conducive to productive —"

I pressed my hand up to his mouth. "I've had about enough of Professor Mullins."

His eyes looked hurt. Beneath the tips of my fingers, I felt the coolness of his lips, the soft hush of his breath. I lowered my hand and opened the door. "But I'm glad I came and found you."

"I want to help," he said as I turned. "It's not easy fighting miracles."

"No," I said. "It pretty much sucks." I hopped out and slammed the creaky door. I started walking, not looking back, but I didn't hear him pull away until I was halfway down the drive. Kicking at the gravel, I thought about Jeff's words: *fighting miracles.*

The truck wasn't back yet, so I knew the house would be empty. Up on the porch, something on the swing caught my eye. I thought at first it was a Pennysaver or some advertisement, but as I stepped closer, I recognized it: It was one of Daniel's coverless comics. Resting on top of the comic were a couple of small sticks. The two twigs had been tied with a pine needle to form the shape of a cross. I picked up this strange talisman, turned it over and back. On the first page of the comic, Superman stood before the entrance to the Fortress of Solitude. This was the one Daniel had been reading up at St. Jude's. He must have dropped it in all the excitement.

I spun around quick, scanned what I could see of the compound, squinting into the tree line for movement. But there was nothing. I snapped the cross into pieces, tossed them over the side of the porch. Then, acting calm as I could, I opened the front door and went inside, but once I shut the door behind me, I double locked it. I stayed behind the curtains and stared into the forest, and even though I couldn't see anything suspicious, I felt the truth in my bones. Somewhere out there, that Scarecrow was watching.

CHAPTER FIVE

When my mother finally got home from the Abernathys', she was surprised to find me lying on the couch in the main house. I was flipping through the course catalog for Lock Haven, mostly as a way to keep distracted. I didn't stop looking when I heard her come in.

"How was your day?" she asked behind me.

I laid the catalog on my chest. "Where's Daniel?"

"It's near dusk. He went down to the salt lick."

I stood up and dropped the catalog on the couch. "He shouldn't be out there by himself."

"I don't like that tone, Ann. He's down there alone all the time. Can't we have five minutes when we're not fighting?"

I walked past her into the kitchen. From the window, I could see Daniel down below, sitting on a fallen tree about twenty feet from a chunk of salt we put out to attract deer. They come early in the morning or just before the sun goes down. "How were things over at the Abernathys'? Was Volpe there?"

She opened the fridge door and then poured a glass of white wine. "Grace will be in bed for a few more days. She was delighted to see Daniel."

"Of course she was."

"Daniel got to hold the baby. You should've seen the smile on that boy's face. We just sat them side by side on the bed, but he was sweet. They asked us to come back tomorrow, first thing."

"You'll be there all day again?"

My mother nodded. "They need our help and Daniel enjoyed being there. Why?"

"Just curious," I told her. The truth was that this came as a great relief. She was planning on skipping church.

Something shifted in the shadows down by Daniel. In the half-light, I couldn't tell what it was. I was about to bolt outside when a deer crept out from behind a pine, leaning its head into the clearing. Timidly, it worked its way toward the salt. Daniel never moved.

My mother stepped up and placed her free hand on my shoulder. In the other she held her thin glass. If I were out there, or my mother, or anybody but Daniel, that deer would never have come so close. She looked out at what I saw and said, "He's such a blessed child."

"He's a great kid," I countered.

My mother squeezed my shoulder and took a sip from her glass. Then she said, "Sylvia. And the Abernathys'. Mayor Wheeler and his wife. They'd like to have a special service at the UCP."

"Special," I said back. I faced her. "Special for what?"

"To give thanks for Miracle. Of course tomorrow is too soon, so they're talking about next Sunday. You could come along," she said quickly. "A lot of people will be there, Ann. Sylvia's apparently put out a few rather ambitious invitations.

It would be nice for us to go, don't you think? As a family, like we used to."

Feeling a bit trapped against the wall, I bumped past her and moved into the more open space of the living room. "I'm going down to sit with Daniel."

She followed right behind me. "I'm your mother, Ann. We can't go through life not talking to each other."

I stopped and turned. "This God the Abernathys are so crazy to thank, this would be the same one who let Gabriella wander onto the ice and drown in the lake, right? The same God who took away their second child before it was even born? But now that they've done enough groveling or tithing or whatever, well, they get to have this baby. A consolation prize maybe. This is the God we're talking about, right?"

She slapped my cheek, hard enough to turn my face. "That's for blasphemy," she explained. "I love you dearly, but you're still my daughter. Now let's speak plainly. This has nothing to do with the Abernathys."

I felt the warm skin of my cheek. "Sure thing," I said. "I don't care about them. I care about Daniel and the Holy Roller boneheads who think he's something he isn't."

My mother sighed. "You know, I've been silly enough to be hopeful lately. That night at the Abernathys, I saw you smile when the baby was born. Your old smile. And these last few days, I've been thinking that this, whatever's happening now, could be a whole new chance for you, Ann. A chance to come back."

"Maybe I don't want to come back."

Again she shook her head and gave me that familiar look of disappointment.

"That crazy guy from St. Jude's stopped by," I said. I pointed to the Superman comic on the coffee table next to the Lock Haven catalog. "Left something on the porch for Daniel."

"You saw this man, here on our property?" she asked.

"Hold it. You think I'm lying?"

She took a sip of her wine and tried to act like she wasn't upset. "I think you're very angry and confused. How do you know Daniel didn't leave it there?"

I pictured that weird cross, which I now regretted breaking. She'd never believe me. "I just know," I said.

"Like you know the people at the church are all crazies?" My mother stared at me, hard-eyed, waiting for an answer.

"Go ahead and say it," I told her.

"Say what?"

"'Just like your father.' I know it's what you're thinking."

"It's a dangerous thing to presume, Ann."

"Great. So tell me I'm wrong."

But instead of answering, my mother turned away and walked back to the window, looking down on Daniel as the last of the light began to leave the sky. I grabbed the course catalog and headed for the trail to my cabin. But then I worried that maybe the Scarecrow really was out there in the dark somewhere, so I swung around the side of the house, quiet as could be. When I rounded the back corner, there were two deer now, each within an arm's reach of Daniel. I froze where I was but still they startled, ears flipping up, eyes flashing to mine, spindly legs springing them back into the forest. Daniel turned and said, "What'd you do that for?"

"Sorry, Little Man. I just wanted to see how your day went."

"Not so good," he said. "Mr. Abernathy made me a hot dog for dinner but they didn't have any ketchup."

"Bummer."

I walked to my brother's side and rubbed my hand over his hair. I had the urge to ask if they'd wanted him to pray.

"All that baby does is sleep and eat."

"She'll play when she gets older."

"Was I little like that?"

I nodded, thinking of all the nights he slept cuddled next to me in my bed. He was warm and smelled so clean. "Sometimes you ate so many peas that your poop was green."

"Gross."

I held my nose. "Tell me about it. I had to clean those diapers."

"Thanks," he offered.

"My pleasure," I said. And really, it was true. Those days before he fell into the ground felt like a fantasy now. Back then, my most serious problems were school projects, chores around the compound, and being a good big sister.

"I could hear you and Mom fighting," Daniel said.

I glanced up at the house. "We weren't fighting," I told him.

"Sure you were. You're mad at her and she's mad at you. Don't lie, Andi."

"Look," I said. "Sometimes grown-ups have a hard time working things out."

He nodded, like this was a fact he knew already. Then he pressed one of his sneaker toes into the ground and said, "Are you gonna leave?"

I grabbed him by the shoulders and pulled him in to me, squeezed both arms around him. "No, I'm not gonna leave. I'm your big sister and I love you."

With his face pressed sideways, he said, "Didn't Dad love me too?"

I felt a sickness in my gut. "Of course Dad loved you. He loved all of us."

"Then why did he go?"

I thought of all the reasons I'd come up with since my father's departure: that he was weak, a coward; that he figured we'd be happier without him; that he didn't think the same way as the people around here; that the place, or maybe the curse of Irene McGinley, just drove him crazy. But I didn't believe any of these things, so I told my brother the absolute truth. "I don't know, Daniel. I just don't know."

After that I walked him around to the porch and sent him inside for his bath. I headed down to my cabin but, rather than getting ready for bed myself, I tugged my sleeping bag from the closet and grabbed a pillow. I pulled an old aluminum bat from a hall closet, then marched back up to the main house. I dragged one of the Adirondack chairs to the corner of the porch, giving me a view of the road, the cabins, and the lake. Later, I planned on rolling out my bag by the front door so the Scarecrow would have to step over my body if he came back for Daniel. For now though, I laid the aluminum bat on my lap and kept watch as long as the fading sun would allow, and my thoughts floated back to the summer before my father left us.

After my brother's rescue, things seemed to get stranger week by week. I don't know who first used the term *Miracle Boy*, but pretty soon it was all over the TV. Even before Daniel was released from the hospital, he and that miner were on magazine covers and some guy from Hollywood called to say he wanted to buy the rights to make a movie.

The very first Sunday following the accident, while my dad was up at St. Jude's with Daniel still in intensive care, my mother and I attended a standing-room-only service at the UCP. By then there were a dozen reporters in town. Volpe was probably one of them, though I don't remember seeing her. Mrs. Wheeler let them all set up their cameras by Mrs. Krupchak's piano, so they had a good view and everything. The citizens, packed in the pews and spilling into the aisles, applauded when we walked in, and everyone was weeping with joy through the opening songs.

It'd been decades since the UCP had an official leader like normal churches. Instead, each Sunday a different member of Paradise would read from the Bible and reflect on Christ's will. There'd be another song or two, and then we'd move on to the main event, when people would offer their testimony.

The testimony at the Universal Church of Paradise was divided into two parts: the praises and the petitions. The praises always came first, where people shared their good news and thanked God for the week's blessings. As a child, the praises had been my favorite part of the service. I'd wait my turn and say something good like, *Thank you, God, for my new baby brother,* or *Praise God for the B-plus I got on my report about FDR.* Whatever. Surrounded by so much good fortune, you had the impression that the world was simply a wonderful place, like nothing could ever go wrong. That summer day when it was just me and my mother, the praises were just one after the next different versions of "Thank you, God, for saving our Daniel." To be honest, despite the cameras and the crying and even the *our*, like my brother was community property, none of it really bothered me. Daniel was alive, and I was grateful.

The second half of the testimony was the petitions, when you put your needs before the Lord. There wasn't a real order to who went first, you just had to wait till the spirit moved you. Typically somebody'd get us started with something admittedly minor, like *Protect all our school's athletes as they compete*, or *Guide Christine's studies in France*, but before long people got down to business, pleading *Be with Mayor Wheeler when he goes to the capitol* or *Help Harold Cedars keep clear of that bottle*.

That first service after Daniel's accident, I thought it was appropriate that nobody petitioned God for anything except for blessings for the miners and for Daniel to heal. But then right at the end, Mrs. Braithwaite stood up on her veiny legs. She pushed through to the lectern and lifted her droopy face and glared until everyone fell silent. "Heavenly Father," she began, "help us all to recognize the certain sign of Your work here among us. Help all of us fully appreciate Daniel as Your divine and holy gift."

Well, this caught me by surprise, but everybody else just amen-ed and hallelujah-ed, like the idea of Daniel being a divine gift was something everyone had talked about and accepted for years. I looked up at my mother, and she saw me looking, but she just stared straight ahead at the altar. I knew she wouldn't tell my dad, who generally would take any excuse to skip coming to church.

A couple weeks later, Daniel came home from St. Jude's with his right foot in a tiny blue cast. My parents did interviews on the phone, and people stopped by our house to have their picture taken with him. By now, letters and postcards were arriving from all over America, plus Canada, Mexico, even China. Up in the fairy fort, a construction company filled in Daniel's hole with concrete and then, just for show, moved that fist-shaped boulder over it. The place became a tourist attraction of sorts. Meanwhile, more and more outsiders started attending services at the UCP. For all I know, Scarecrow could've been in one of those crowds. I wouldn't have noticed, distracted as I was.

You see, even Daniel's first return to our church was pretty freaky. The vestibule filled up and then they had to open the outer doors and let people stand in the field. Everyone in the congregation kept grinning and waving at Daniel, even while Emma Guidry read from the Bible. Then during the praises, things got downright weird. Ryan Thomason said, "Thank you, Lord, for the plentiful fish this summer. And thank you for Daniel." Lisell Williams flashed peace signs to everyone and said, "My carpal tunnel was getting so I couldn't work. Now it's flat gone. Thank you, Lord. And thank you for Daniel." Through thin tears, Deidre LaMont said, "Those nightmares have finally left me, Jesus. Praise your name. And thank you for Daniel."

In some strange way, every blessing — no matter how great or small — became connected to my brother. Meanwhile, he just sat between my parents, picking at the stuffing in his cast. Dad squirmed in his seat, clearly uncomfortable, and what happened during the petitions only made things worse. Rita Solomon stood up and turned toward Daniel directly. "Christ Jesus," she said. "You saved one son of Paradise. Please just let me know that Cody's still alive." Her teenage boy had run off to join a band in

New York. Hank Grenke, just down the pew from us, fixed his eyes on Daniel and said, "Lord, you know my secret shame. Take it away from me, let me lay my burden down." And Miriam Sinclair, usually so timid you couldn't hear her, shouted out as she faced my brother, "My cousin needs a gift like Daniel's." She explained that the surgeons couldn't remove all the cancer from her cousin's brain and that she couldn't handle much more chemo. Just like with the praises, every petition grew associated with Daniel. Even though the believers were talking to God, they were staring at my brother.

The next week, over my dad's protests, my mother encouraged Daniel to at least fold his hands and look prayerful while his name was being mentioned. He'd twist his fat fingers together and bend his head, but at three, it was just a game to him. He had no idea he was being asked to intercede with God.

Over the course of a month or so, with so many petition-wishes, word came that some were indeed granted. The praises began to fill up with reports of miraculous success. Cody Solomon called home asking for money. The Bradfords finally had their application for adoption approved. Charlotte Dean's bursitis cleared up. Mr. Hogan's bad ear, which everybody in town knew about, was suddenly just fine. Eamon Littleton got that new job in Binghamton. Elizabeth Manfred threw away her epilepsy pills and the seizures did not return. And one Sunday, Miriam Sinclair walked all the way to the lectern to announce that her cousin's latest CAT scan showed no signs of a tumor. The doctors had never seen anything like it.

When Miriam announced that, the congregation broke into glorious applause. Beaming and smiling, praising God with shouts of joy, everyone turned to Daniel, now held tight in my mother's arms. My dad gave me a look of something like disgust, and I felt something I'd never felt before in church: fear. Week by week through that summer, thanks to nothing but a bunch of coincidences, the citizens of Paradise decided that my brother was more than just lucky. They came to believe he was blessed, miraculous.

That summer, Action Water Thrill Ride City was in its second year, and buses came up from Philly and down from New York. Because of the national publicity of Daniel's rescue, people knew about our town, and quite a few drove all this way in part to get a glimpse of the Miracle Boy. Of course, they'd spend the day and enjoy a couple meals, browse through the antique shops and pick up a few souvenirs — bumper stickers, a T-shirt, a magnet for the fridge. That year's Paradise Days was the biggest on record. It was easy to believe Mayor Wheeler's slogan: Paradise is on the rise.

But then late one August afternoon, not long after Jeff had taken off for Penn State, Volpe came by the house on that silly red scooter. She brought news that Mrs. Bundower had taken a turn for the worse. You already know what happened that night, how they expected Daniel to keep that dying woman alive, how he ended up trembling in the closet. The night Mrs. Bundower died, something inside me started to shift.

A couple of weeks later, an angler renting Cabin Three came banging on the door of the main house. Dad was making me scrambled eggs and we answered the door together. We followed him through the pines and hemlocks, and halfway down the trail we hit the smell, like tuna left out too long. By the time we got to the lake, the stench was so strong that I was gagging and my stomach muscles were clenching up. The bloated corpses of maybe a hundred fish — rock bass, trout, sunnies — were all floating on the surface of the water. They were openmouthed and wide-eyed, as if they were staring at whoever killed them. Along the rocky shoreline, dozens more rotted on their sides like tiny beached whales. Some of the fish were still sucking at air or twitching their shiny tails. My dad took off his baseball cap and scratched the back of his head. The fisherman renting the cabin asked about a refund.

It wasn't just by our dock — all over the lake, the fish were dead or dying. As the morning came on and the sun went to work on those bodies, the odor drove vacationing families from their rented cabins, sent hunters upstream and over the ridge. We closed our windows against the stench. People threw away the fish they'd caught and frozen to eat in the winter. In a day or two, even the hardiest sportsmen had moved north, upriver past the bridge to where the fish still thrived. The tourists, with all their money, pretty much disappeared. And the specialists descended. There were scientists from Fish and Wildlife, a team of graduate researchers from Hershey, and an environmental group from Vermont. Articles in the *Five Mountains Gazetteer* explained the scientists' findings, always using phrases like "optimum water quality," "conflicting data," and "anomalous readings." We were assured that nothing in the water could harm humans, but no one wanted to risk it. Something just seemed wrong with dipping your body in water where nothing lived. It was so strange in the late summer, on beautiful sunny days, to see no boats on the lake. By the end of August, the older folks in town began to cross themselves and say, "Rest in peace, Irene McGinley. Leave us be."

Up at the UCP, the out-of-town visitors thinned out and services grew somber. No one was praising much, and the petitions were mostly all variations of the same theme — *bring back the fish*. One week Mr. Abernathy read from the Bible about there being a time for every purpose under God's heaven, but we all wondered what purpose God had in killing our town. All the while, people stared harder and harder at Daniel, like somehow he had something to do with it. It had been just four months since he was rescued from the ancient well, and a month or so since Mrs. Bundower died.

Everything came to a head one Sunday morning in September, at the beginning of my junior year. My family was a little late, and all four of us hustled across the grass parking lot and mounted the front steps. I opened the doors to a strange sight. A bunch of parishioners were standing in the vestibule: the Wheelers, the Abernathys, Mrs. Braithwaite, the Cullen sisters, maybe a dozen others, the ones who believed most in the curse of Irene McGinley and the miraculous powers of my brother. Behind them, through the second set of doors, I could hear singing and Mrs. Krupchak's piano. As my family moved inside, they turned toward us with cold, hard eyes. Mrs. Wheeler stepped forward, and my dad bent over and picked up Daniel.

He asked, "Everything all right here, Judy?"

"We've talked about this," she answered. "And we're all agreed."

"About what?"

She lifted her chin at Daniel. "He needs to ask God to bring back the fish."

My mother stepped in between Dad and the group, rubbing

her hands and forcing a smile. "Daniel prays the same as you. He prays for the same thing we've all been praying for."

Mrs. Wheeler shook her head. "But nothing's happening. Without the fish, there'll be no Paradise. Don't you see? The boy has to pray harder."

Daniel buried his face in my dad's shoulder.

"Pray harder?" my dad echoed. "He's three years old." His arms tightened around Daniel. "You people —" he said. "You should have your damn heads examined." Then he turned and kicked open the outside door. As my dad stepped back into the sunlight, I followed, but we both hesitated when we realized my mother wasn't with us. Dad said, "Nancy."

My mother stood in the space between us and the true believers. Behind the second set of doors, the singing stopped. She folded her hands in front of her and looked down at them for a second, and when she looked up again she said, "I'll talk with them, Charles. We shouldn't just leave. Whether you like it or not, we're part of this church, and this church is part of us."

Holding Daniel in his arms, my dad stared at my mother, shook his head, and turned away. The door closed behind him and I was left in that room with all of them silent and waiting. I didn't know what I should do, but I didn't like the way they were looking at me, so I went after my dad, just barely catching him before he tore out of the parking lot in his Jeep.

That night was the first time I heard my parents really fighting. Not just disagreeing, but fighting. They yelled at each other in the kitchen, catching themselves when their voices rose too high. Even when I crept out to the head of the stairs, I couldn't make out the words, but I didn't really need to. The sharp tones, the long silences, they said it all.

On the way back to my room, I worried that maybe they'd woken Daniel like they'd woken me. I stepped into his pitch-black room and heard this crazy rambling, a rush of words that didn't make sense: "merciful God please plentiful gratitude holy forgive redeemer the fish forgive us our weakness please please oh please." I snapped on the light but that didn't stop his ranting. His eyeballs rolled beneath his lids, like they do when you're dreaming but faster. And the sweat beaded up on his forehead and his hands were clenched together so tight in prayer his fingernails had nearly drawn blood. "Daniel!" I shouted, and I shook him by the shoulders till he came to. He opened his eyes and saw me and started to cry. I crawled in next to him and held him in my arms. "Listen to me," I said. "None of this is your fault."

He wiped his nose on my shirt. "I ask God for the fish to come back, Andi, I do. How come they won't?"

I took his small face between my hands — his cheeks were hot to the touch — and I aimed his eyes into mine. "Daniel, you ain't special. Everybody's been praying for the fish. Do you understand me? Your prayers don't mean more than anybody else's. No matter what people tell you."

"They think I'm like Superman."

"That's right," I said. "But you're not. *You ain't special.* What happened to Mrs. Bundower — you couldn't stop that. And you can't bring the fish back. Nobody can. Nothing is your fault. Okay? Tell me you understand."

Daniel nodded his head. "Yeah. I understand. It ain't my fault."

"That's right. You're just like everybody else. Say it."

"I'm just like everybody else. I'm not special."

Daniel curled in to me, his back to my chest. I reached over and clicked off his night-light. I stared out the window and watched the moon cross behind the pines and listened to my parents' voices rise and crack. By the time they stopped, the moon had slid from my view. Downstairs, the front door creaked open and snapped shut, and Dad stirred the first few leaves of fall as he left the house, heading for Cabin Five to sleep alone. My mother's footsteps came slowly up the stairs. Across the hall, she opened my door to check on me. A moment later she opened Daniel's door, and her silhouette filled the frame. Even though I looked right at her, the darkness hid my face. But I couldn't read her expression either, so I'm not sure if she knew I was awake. I guess she just wanted to be sure Daniel was with me, because without saying a word she eased the door shut and left us alone.

My dad wouldn't go back to the UCP and he was dead set against Daniel going. Every Sunday meant a battle between my parents, occasionally one with shouts and accusations, but more often the silent warfare of eye rolls, shrugs, and deep sighs. Those days that my mother won, I'd go along to watch over Daniel.

Slowly, my faith began to sour. Especially once the fish died, I came to see the praises for what they really were — a gigantic ass-kissing session. The congregation was just trying to get on God's good side for the petitions. Begging for the fish to come back was one thing, but there were others that suddenly sounded ridiculous, things like *Give comfort to the recently unemployed* or

Help the victims of the hurricane in Florida. These were the petitions that got under my skin, and even to this day I can't quite wrap my brain around them. Did God, all-powerful, all-mighty, have to be reminded to help people who'd had their houses smashed to pieces by a natural disaster? Did we really think that He'd hear our petition and suddenly say, "Whoa, all those people don't have food. Maybe I should help?" What sort of divine being needed to be coerced into kindness and mercy?

In the wake of my dad's big scene at the UCP, no one mentioned Daniel by name. But I caught knowing glances, and I swore that Mr. Hogan deliberately walked along beside us when we left, just so he could brush his fingers across Daniel's hair. After services those Sundays, I'd take Daniel for long hikes in the woods, or we'd ride in the open kayak down to the dam, where we'd go exploring along the rocks.

When we got back, my mother's eyes were always red, and my dad was always down in his cabin watching football. Daniel asked me why Dad wasn't sleeping in his own bed, and I made up a lie about the mattress down in the cabin being better for Dad's bad back. Before the leaves finished falling, Dad was staying down there every night. That October, with the cold coming on, the two of us stacked split logs for the main cabin and his, and as I'd go to bed I'd look out and see the smoke billowing from Cabin Five's chimney. He even stopped eating dinner with the family.

But every morning, I'd come downstairs ready for my run and find him in the kitchen, making strong coffee and flipping through the *Gazetteer.* I knew he was looking for work in the slim classifieds. My mother had inherited the compound outright from her parents along with a little bit of money, so even though our cabins weren't renting, nobody was starving. But when I'd go with Dad around town on odd jobs — replacing Dr. Candeza's water heater, closing down the Hertzogs' swimming pool — I could tell that without steady work, he was going stir-crazy in Paradise. It was there in the far-off look in his eyes when he was driving, the way he'd curse when a rusted nut would snap. My dad and I never discussed any of these weighty matters. Instead, on those quiet winter mornings, we'd talk about track or school or a used snowmobile that somebody was selling cheap in the classifieds. Even after the trouble got worse, we never really talked about the fish, never about Daniel, and never ever about my mother.

Then came the day of the great ice storm. It hadn't snowed at all yet that year, and there was nothing in the forecast. I came downstairs that morning ready to talk with Dad and then go for my jog, but I found the kitchen dark and empty. The tiniest snowflakes floated past the glass doors that led to the porch, dusting the wood white. At a side window, I saw a light on down in Dad's cabin. I slipped on the heavy sweatshirt and wool cap I wore to run, then shuffled through the fresh powder coating the trail. My breath made clouds in the air. I had no gloves, and my fingers went stiff quick. I never knocked on his door, and so I walked uninvited through the cabin to the rear room where he slept. He had his back to me, and two suitcases were open on the bed. I remember a moment when I thought this meant he was coming home. But then he turned to me and I saw his face, unshaven. His eyes were red from lack of sleep.

"What are you doing?" I asked him.

He froze like I'd caught him in the middle of a crime. Glancing at the floor, he said, "It's not you, Andi. Don't ever think this was because of you. I just don't belong here."

"Neither do I," I said.

He looked at me, studying the face that everyone in town said looked just like his.

"Dad," I said. "I'm the same as you."

"No," he said. "You're better than me. You're going to have a better life than mine."

He turned to the closet and went back to putting clothes in the suitcase, as if I'd left the room. I just watched him.

"What about Mom?" I asked. "Don't you love her?"

"She's my wife," he said. "But she believes things I don't. The people around here, I'm just not one of them."

I thought about what I was going to say, and I knew it was wrong and selfish not to ask for Daniel. "Take me with you," I pleaded.

With both hands, he pressed a suitcase closed and snapped it shut. "You and Dan, you're going to stay with your mother. It's better this way. For everybody." He looked at me then, and his dim eyes were heavy with failure and shame. "Trust me, one day this will all make sense." He kissed me on the forehead and picked up the suitcases, walked out the door without looking back.

That's the kind of scene you never forget, even if you try. And just for the record, years later, I'm still waiting for his decision to even start making sense.

I wandered around inside Cabin Five, focusing for some reason on things he'd left behind, and then my eyes landed on the matches on the mantelpiece. I stepped over to the window next to the fireplace and saw my father up above at his Jeep. I reached for the box of matches and pulled one out, scratched it on the sandpaper side, and held the flame to the curtains. The fire covered the window in seconds, and I walked calmly down the steps and into the snow.

I never moved from that spot, not while Dad stretched a garden hose from Cabin Four and began frantically spraying, not when I saw my mother holding Daniel back in the clearing above us, not when the heat raised a sunburn glow on my cheeks. I just stood there watching the gray smoke curl and twist through the pine branches, witness to the destruction I had released.

Even after the roof collapsed and the cabin was lost for sure, Dad kept hosing it. Now and then he'd turn the water on the nearby trees. The flames blackened the chimney's brick, but it stayed standing. Crackling and popping, the wood consumed itself, and barely thirty minutes after I lit that match, what was left of the cabin was smoldering beneath the spray from Dad's hose. He was tending a garden of ash.

All the while, the snow kept coming, and flakes drifted into the gray smoke. I watched. With the heat gone, the wetness froze on the trees, encasing the pines in thin ice, an omen of the freak winter weather that was coming Paradise's way.

None of this made my dad change his escape plan. He climbed into his red Jeep and drove off into the worst storm Paradise had ever seen. I watched him leave from my bedroom window upstairs, and after he disappeared into the icy snow, I felt entirely alone. That's when I decided that nobody was listening to the problems of mere mortals, that even if there was a heavenly father, He didn't much care about His children. We'd been abandoned. Betrayed and bitter, I vowed I'd never pray again.

In the years since that day, I've wondered why I burned Cabin Five. Maybe I was angry at it for the role it had played in the disintegration of my parents' marriage. Maybe I wanted my father to know that once he left, he couldn't come back. Maybe I just went a little crazy. But it didn't do any good. It was too little, too late. I'd failed Daniel by not stopping Dad from leaving, just like I'd failed him by letting him fall down that hole. I'd failed him again by not standing up to the Jesus freaks who thought him miraculous. And now that this threat had returned, I sure wasn't going to make the same mistake. Sitting in that Adirondack chair, keeping one eye out for the Scarecrow with a bat across my lap, I imagined the next Sunday and that special prayer service Volpe had arranged. How everybody would know he'd be there, and how the people's eyes would shine when they gazed on my brother and poured out their petitions.

Remembering all that happened with Cabin Five and my dad brought an idea to my mind: If Volpe and the Abernathys and the Wheelers didn't have a building, they couldn't have their prayer service. And if they didn't have that prayer service, Daniel might stay safe. Listening to the darkness of the woods, it occurred to me that for my brother's sake, I might have to burn down the only church in Paradise.

CHAPTER SIX

I woke early in the morning to birdsong and a stiff and achy back, the price you pay, I guess, for a night in an Adirondack chair. Gradually light came into the world, first as a glow crowning the mountains across the lake, then as beams splitting through the woods around me. I watched the show, in no particular rush to get moving with my plans for the day. Of course I knew arson was a crime, and the fact that my potential target was a holy building occupied by the spirit of God likely qualified it as an unpardonable sin. But wouldn't it be worse to let Daniel get hurt? Since my father left, I hadn't prayed — not once — but it crossed my mind to ask for divine guidance. But I doubted that Jesus would give an approving nod to a pyromaniac, no matter how noble my intention. All night long, I'd tried to think of different options, but nothing had occurred to me. So, with no other choices and with the sun high enough to light the forest floor, I started my Sunday, thinking maybe I'd save my brother with spite and with fire.

Inside the house, I heard my mother in the kitchen, probably getting things ready for their trip to the Abernathys. Some part of me secretly wanted to be going with them again, and not just to go and visit the baby, but next week, even to the UCP. I missed the easy comfort of believing that everything happens for a reason. Blind faith removes the hard choices of your life. I decided to not even go inside and say good morning. When they couldn't find me, they'd assume I was out jogging.

I headed for the shed. Inside, the dim lightbulb seemed about to go dead, so it was hard to see except for the hazy morning glow forcing its way through a grimy window. Dust floated in the air, and I picked my way around the riding mower and a green bicycle with a busted front wheel. I fished through one of my dad's old cigar boxes, shoving aside spare keys and odd batteries until my fingers found a book of matches. Just to be sure, I struck one and it flared instantly. I also cracked open Dad's toolbox and took hold of the familiar red pocketknife. Over the years since he left, I'd used it on plenty of chores, but I always replaced it. I never carried it around like it was mine.

Five minutes later I was in the kayak, shoving off from the dock and paddling south on smooth water.

Like most days at that point, there was hardly anybody on the lake. Over on the west side, a couple kids were splashing in inner tubes just off their dock. Behind me to the north, up close to Roosevelt Park, the sharp white triangle of a single sailboat cruised along.

When I paddled past Cedars Marina, there was no sign that anyone was awake yet. I wondered if Jeff was lying on that bumpy bed, maybe thinking of me. I stayed near the shoreline till McGinley's Cove, where I veered out into the open water. As I passed the mouth of the horseshoe-shaped cove, I glanced in at the sheer rock face of the cliff. From the surely haunted cave along the base to the Lookout above was a two-hundred-foot drop. Rocks in the water made the cove impossible to boat in, and the stony shoreline offered no beach. Supposedly, this was where the bodies of Irene McGinley's boys were found after they drowned, so even before Michelle Kirkpatrick drove her car off the edge on prom night, most people avoided the place. As kids, Jeff and I had climbed down there more than a few times, picked our way along the jagged rocks, dared each other to go deeper and deeper into that cave.

On the lake, I tried to forget about where I was and where I was going. Instead I concentrated on the rowing, the reach-dig-pull of the paddles' rhythm, which fell as it always did into a cadence like running. But every so often, my cheeks would warm with heat and I'd imagine the UCP engulfed in a pillar of flame. The wrath of Anderson Grant.

Ten minutes farther south, I rounded a bend and came into view of the corpse of Action Water Thrill Ride City. Mayor Wheeler announced that dumb name after he convinced the city council to give the land to an amusement park company in hopes of luring tourists. This was just after the new highway aimed them all away from us. Eighteen months later the park opened up with a day of free admission to everyone in Paradise, and of course my parents brought me and Daniel, then just a toddler. Gayle went all out and ran a full front-page story in the *Gazetteer*, complete with an aerial photograph. In the back, skirting the forest's edge, the photo showed the asphalt loop of Thunder Road, where you could race a whining car in circles, and the Around the World in 18 Holes miniature golf course. Along the lake was a basketball court–size sandbox that led up to the kiddie pool. Behind it were three huge slides (painted red, white, and blue — honest) that sloped down into the giant wave pool. But the main attraction, the hallmark ride that was supposed to bring them in from other states and other time zones and make us some kind of international tourist destination, rose from the center of the park: the Twin Terrors, a pair of hundred-foot, tubular green slides that curled in to each other. The day the park opened, everything was shiny and new, and Mayor Wheeler cut the ceremonial ribbon and announced, "Paradise is on the rise!" And we all believed him.

But just five years later, by the time I was paddling past in the kayak, the park was long-since dead, ravaged by the same ice storm that my dad drove off into, the one that freed Samson and did in the Black Hole Bridge. Through the cyclone fence, I saw that crabgrass and weeds had claimed the sandbox, the big blue slide leaned precariously, and the red and white ones had collapsed, leaving forty-foot stairways that led nowhere. Somehow both Twin Terrors survived, but now there was so much mold and mossy growth along the sides of the green tubes that they resembled monstrous filthy snakes emerging from the earth. On the concrete wall of the Snax Stand, somebody had spray painted what all of us had thought at one point or another: THIS IS PARADISE?

After I passed the park, I could see the dam in the distance, but there was nothing else to distract me. I found myself thinking more about that book of matches in my pocket.

The UCP was built in a clearing that faces the lake, complete with a rolling grassy hill that leads right down to the water's edge. But since I didn't want to be discovered, I started steering the kayak toward land well before I reached holy ground. I found a place a hundred yards north where some branches draping the shoreline would provide enough cover. After I drove the kayak's tip onto the rocky bank, I scanned for witnesses. Once I was sure no one was around, I grounded the kayak and started into the woods.

After I hiked up the incline for a few minutes, the white cross atop the steeple became clear through the trees. Next I saw the slate roof, and beneath it the white wooden walls with their slim, stained glass windows. The grass parking lot, which would fill later with cars for the three o'clock service, was empty.

I knew the big wooden doors out front would be locked, and even trying them would put me in plain sight of anyone passing by on the lake. So I broke from the woods back behind the building, shimmied an oil drum used for burning leaves up to the bathroom window, flipped it over, and then climbed up. Unfolding the blade of my father's pocketknife, I pried the lock and broke into the house of God.

I squeezed through the window and had to put my hands on the floor, which was gross. As I stood and turned toward the door, somebody else moved in the shadows. I flinched, and the figure in the shadows flinched too. I stared into my shady reflection in the mirror above the sink and shook my head. I washed my hands and headed for the door.

In the dark hallway, I inched along the wall with one arm out in front of me like a blind man. In the years since I'd been inside the UCP, I'd forgotten that peaceful smell — the pleasant blend of candles, mothballs, and incense. Once I reached the sacristy, dull light leaked beneath a doorway, and I shuffled toward it. And when I pushed through the door and stepped out behind the altar, the main room seemed huge, like a cavern. Early morning sunlight slanted through the stained glass, bathing the pews in purple and yellow and red. Dust hovered in the tinted brightness.

I found myself drawn to the lectern, where as a child I used to stand on a metal milk crate so I could read from the Bible. I remembered my mother helping me learn how to pronounce "abominable" by drawing a picture of a bull with a stick of dynamite inside it. Usually children read only at Christmas or Easter, but I was kind of a special case. Who knows why, but people said I had a calling to serve the Lord. Don't laugh. There was a time when the idea didn't seem so crazy.

Alone in the church, I wrapped my fingers around the worn wooden edges of the lectern and looked out over the empty pews, but I saw them standing there, all the citizens of Paradise. Mayor Wheeler and his wife in the front, my mother and Daniel right behind them. My father. The McDormits and the twin Cullen sisters. Jeff Cedars and his family. The MacKenns. The Zanines. Lute Moody. And if all of them were really there, right then in that moment, what sermon would I have preached to them, with hate in my heart and those matches in my pocket?

I stepped away from the lectern and went down to the pew my family always occupied. Leo told me that faith is about believing when you have no reason to believe, but looking back at all of it, I don't blame myself for deciding that I was wasting my time. The truth is that my faith left town with my father. After he drove off, I vowed I'd never pray again. Even if there was a God, He was no friend of mine.

Of course, feeling this way was one thing; lighting a church on fire was another. Something was holding me back, maybe doubt in my plan, maybe a lingering flicker of faith. But I took a deep breath and decided that it had to be done. The only question was how. I looked around and figured my best bet would be to gather up all the hymnals and make a pile up on the wooden altar. Thinking of that image, an altar I once considered holy aflame, it just seemed wrong. So instead of collecting all the songbooks, I sat there in silent reflection, and it's true, I felt tempted again to pray for guidance.

When I first heard the whiny rattling sound outside, I took it for a motorboat out on the water. But then it got louder, and I wondered if somebody wasn't trolling the woods on a four-wheeler. I walked toward the front doors, thinking to peer out on the grass field stretching to the lake. Before I could, though, a huge shape cruised by the side of the church. Its shadow through the stained glass windows made me think of a whale. Whatever it was swung around to the front door and the motor cut off. Immediately I heard voices. I dropped down and slipped beneath a pew, belly to the carpeted floor.

A key worked in the front double doors and then one swung open, allowing the morning light to fall upon the floor. Two sets of shoes came in: one comfortable sneakers, the others heavy boots, the kind you might see on a serious hiker. They passed by me and stopped a few pews up. Sylvia Volpe's voice said, "Welcome to our little church." By its location, I knew she was the sneakers.

"Every church is the size it should be," the boots said. His voice was deep and rich, calm too.

"It's not too small?" Volpe asked.

"If people fill the pews, we'll open those doors. They can stand on the grass."

"Of course," Volpe said. She was clearly delighted. "I think I can rent a tent over in Hawley."

"No need," the boots said. "I have one in the back of the bus somewhere."

Now the sound of the motor was familiar and the whale shape made sense.

"It's old but it'll keep the rain off peoples' heads if need be. I've had it forever. Used to use it all the time back in my more active days."

There was an awkward silence, one even Volpe seemed to recognize. She cleared her throat. "You know," she said, "I saw you years ago. I was just a teenager."

"Really?" the boots said. "I'll be."

"Outside of Cleveland, a muddy hillside. You preached on the Beatitudes."

Boots laughed. "I remember that hill, but not the sermon. Guess I'm getting old."

They were quiet again for a few moments.

"It was kind of you to invite me here, Sylvia, truly. I really don't travel much at all anymore, and it's been good to be out on the road again. It gets the blood moving."

"The honor is mine. I'm pleased the church will meet your needs."

"It's a fine church, just lovely. But between you and me, I've always preferred being outdoors. Makes me feel closer to God. I was up in the woods the other day, down by that park. I walked up and found the clearing where the boy fell in the well."

"The fairy fort?"

"It's a special place, touched by God. I met some interesting people up there, and they felt it too. If it weren't quite so difficult to get to, I'd try to talk you into having a service up there."

"I could speak to the council and see if we —"

"No, no. When a local church makes itself available, I always use it. Or I used to, back when I did this kind of thing more."

"Whatever you think is best, Reverend."

"You're most kind," he said.

I felt foolish clutching those matches now, realizing that even if I did burn the church to the ground, these people would go right on with their Holy Roller services. They'd just have it out in the field or on the lawn at Roosevelt Park. And I'd be watching like the Grinch looking down at Whoville on Christmas morning.

The two sets of shoes moved past me again, stepping on the sunlight and heading for the door. Volpe asked, "Should I seek out some people who might benefit, if Daniel feels moved to share God's love at the service?"

I wanted to kick her shins. She wanted to round up sick folks for Daniel to heal. This was exactly the kind of crap I'd been afraid of all along, that he'd be pressured into performing miracles he couldn't.

"I don't think that's called for," the Reverend said, surprising me. "In any group of people, there will always be those in need. We will gather to give thanks and offer our praise. I've learned to let God take it from there."

Volpe said, "Whatever you think is best," but I could tell by her tone she wasn't pleased.

The Reverend didn't seem to notice. "I'd like to meet the family before the service. I understand the boy lives with his mother."

"Nancy's been through a great deal. After Daniel's accident, her husband, a man of slim faith, left her."

"So she's alone, then?"

"She has another child, a teenage daughter who is causing, well, complications."

"That would seem to be the role of teenagers in our world."

He chuckled and I couldn't help but smile. It was his warm voice, I convinced myself, that made it hard to dislike him.

"Reverend," Volpe said, "have you ever considered coming out of retirement full-time? The world has lost its way. It needs men of great conviction."

"I'm old, Sylvia," the man said. "Old and tired. Besides, preachers do their work on TV now. No one goes to tent revivals."

"If they knew you were available, many would invite you to their churches. Halls can be rented."

"You sound like a manager." The old man laughed. "The whole notion is tempting, but we know the source of temptation. It would take a great sign to get me back on the road. Something truly extraordinary."

"Daniel is extraordinary."

This froze my blood and caught that preacher's attention. He took a big breath and said, "So you say."

Volpe pressed her advantage. "The two of you together, you'd make a powerful team for the Lord."

The preacher rocked on his boots and I could tell his mind was working. Finally he said, "I'm open to the will of God. We'll pray for His guidance."

They kept talking as they walked out, but I couldn't hear what else they said. As I slipped out from under the pew, my mind rolled through what sounded like their plans for Daniel. They wanted to take my brother away, drive him off in that white bus and go on a nutjob miracle tour of America. I pictured the

Reverend's tent set up in a field somewhere, with Daniel inside, fevered and pale, waiting for those in need of healing.

Since Volpe locked the church doors behind her, I had to crawl out through the same window I'd broken into. As I hiked back to my hidden kayak, the matches felt silly in my hand. The whole notion of burning down the church seemed childish, unsophisticated. I needed a more subtle strategy.

Paddling north on the lake, I thought about some of the things Jeff had said. He was right about one thing: The problem was that I had to find a way to make folks stop believing. Something had to happen, like in those stories I'd read of defrauded miracle workers. Somehow I needed to convince everyone that Daniel was a fake, a hoax like the Scarecrow thought he might be.

All of this was settling into my head as I passed McGinley's Cove. And I stopped paddling and laid back, let the kayak drift, and listened to the silence of the lake. I heard the water gently sloshing up against the rocks on the shoreline. I saw the huge open mouth of the cave and the cliff that rises up two hundred feet, to the Lookout that Michelle Kirkpatrick sailed her car over on prom night, wearing the dress Mrs. Bundower sewed for her. I don't believe much in visions, but as I was imagining what that must have looked like, I could almost see the car racing over the edge. Something was wrong with the image, and I saw that the car wasn't Michelle Kirkpatrick's, and the driver was me. As I floated on the water, the Anti-Miracle Plan came to me, fully formed. I knew what I had to pull off before that church service next Sunday and I knew exactly how my hoax would work. Best of all, I finally felt confident in what I needed to do next: get a car and find some blood.

CHAPTER SEVEN

The very afternoon of the Sunday when I had my Anti-Miracle vision, while my mother and Daniel were again over at the Abernathys' and the true believers of Paradise attended the regular weekly service in the church I hadn't burned down, I called Jeff on the phone and asked if he'd help me pick out a decent used car.

"What do you need a car for?" he asked.

He was anxious, no doubt, concerned that this might be the first step in my fledgling career as a kidnapper. But the question was inevitable, one my mother would surely ask too, so I had a lie ready. "Getting back and forth to Lock Haven. I'll come home some weekends, help out around the compound."

There was a pause while Jeff decided whether or not to believe me. "Can't do much on a Sunday," he said. "Nobody's open. How about tomorrow?"

"You're not too busy getting set for Paradise Days?" Opening festivities were scheduled for the end of the week.

"My dad can do without me for a few hours."

Jeff said he'd come by for me about ten and we hung up. I know as much about cars as Jeff does, probably more. If he had guessed that I was lying about needing his help or my reason for wanting a car, I couldn't tell. The truth of course was that any car

I did get had no chance of ever making it to Lock Haven, or anywhere else other than McGinley's Cove. As far as Jeff goes, I just wanted to see him.

Monday morning when Jeff pulled in, Daniel and I were on the front porch, studying a spiderweb we'd found in the railing.

"There's a fly all wrapped up," Daniel told Jeff. "But we can't find the spider."

"Maybe he's taking a walk."

My mother came out, holding her third cup of coffee with two hands and blowing across the top of it. Jeff snatched off his Penn State baseball cap and nodded earnestly. "Morning, Mrs. Grant."

"Hello, Jeff. It's good to see you again." Her voice was sincere, and I could tell she was pleased that Jeff, a stabilizing force in the life of her erratic daughter, had reappeared on the scene.

"Don't buy anything today," my mother said to me. "I may be able to help you out."

"I don't need any money," I told her. Over the last few years, between my time at the *Gazetteer* and handyman jobs around town, I'd saved up nearly a thousand dollars, plenty for a car with the minimal requirements I needed.

"Have you thought about the insurance?" she asked. "You'll have to pay that every month."

Daniel scooted down the steps, away from the tension, and Jeff flopped his hat back on his head as he followed. I hadn't considered insurance because I wouldn't need the car for more than a week, and given my true intentions, I was pretty sure taking out insurance would be fraud. But I couldn't tell her that. "I'll get a part-time job up at school," I said.

"You should focus on your classes," my mother said. "You buy the car. I'll pay for the insurance."

I cocked a sideways glance at her, wondering what she was up to. The night before, she'd tried to talk me out of the whole thing, telling me I should save the money, that she and Daniel could drive up and get me whenever I wanted. Now she seemed eager to help. I didn't say no, but we both understood my silence to mean I accepted her offer. Staring over my shoulder and holding her coffee, my mother smiled. I turned and together we watched Daniel and Jeff peeling bark from a fallen branch, searching for signs of life.

As we rolled north on Roosevelt Road, Jeff suggested that we drive up to Hawley or even the Auto Mile over by the mall in Scranton. I explained that dealerships are rip-offs, then unfolded a week-old *Gazetteer* classifieds page from my back pocket. I'd highlighted a half dozen cars for sale, all local, and already called to get the addresses. Jeff kept his eyes on the road and was quiet, and I realized only then that I might have hurt his feelings. Guys, I've figured out, like to be the ones who make decisions. Maybe he'd had some bigger plan, like getting something to eat at the Applebee's in Hawley. We'd driven there once during my sophomore year, just after Jeff got his license.

"How about we just hit a few of these first?" I offered. "Then get some lunch and go from there?"

Nobody but me would have noticed the slight smile this brought out, but I could tell that, indeed, he saw our time together as a kind of date, and if I'm to be honest, I guess I did too. "Sounds good," he said. "Where to?"

The first two addresses were both busts. Fred Shoemaker's Volvo, hiding sheepishly in his garage, needed headlights and a brake job. At the second stop, Marty Kipplewick showed us his mom's Ford, in pristine condition except for the huge V in the front bumper. Mrs. Kipplewick was slowly losing her eyesight to macular degeneration, and she apparently hadn't seen a fire hydrant when she went to park on the grass at a garage sale. While Jeff and I inspected her car, she stood in a window on the second floor of her home, looking down on us with a neck brace and no expression. I wondered if she could see us at all.

The route to the third house brought us alongside one edge of Roosevelt Park, and through the pines I could make out plenty of activity on the great lawn. In the far parking lot, by the hookups for the RVs, that white school bus sat like a sphinx. I felt the urge to tell Jeff about the reverend with the hiking boots and the full extent of my plans. But he was the one who spoke. Apparently noticing where my attention was focused, he said, "Folks around town are calling them Pilgrims."

I turned to him. "Calling who Pilgrims?"

"The ones living in the park."

He looked at me and I stared back.

"I figured you'd heard about this. At first, everybody thought they were just the usual early bird potheads in town for the festival, or some of the New Agers who can't get enough of the fairy fort. But that's not the case, according to the crowd up at the Dog Bar last night."

"Spit it out, would you?"

"A lot of those people camped out in the park, the Pilgrims — they came here on account of Daniel."

I whispered, "Shit," and looked back at the field, though now it was far behind us. "How many are there?"

"Don't know for sure. Some say a hundred. They're going into the lake, Andi. Baptizing themselves."

"Hang on now. Who's saying all this?"

"Candace Hoffstetler. And Tommy."

In high school, Candace started a rumor that she was pregnant just to get some attention. As for Tommy Wirkus, if he was at the Dog Bar, he was drinking and probably trying to hit on Candace. "Sounds like a bunch of crap to me. Freaking Pilgrims."

"Tommy heard it from Volpe. She's been down there to the park and talked to them."

I scratched my forehead. Maybe kidnapping Volpe would solve my problems. "Now I believe this story even less."

"Don't snap at me. I'm just telling you what I heard."

I told Jeff I just wanted to get on to the next car.

Frank Dettweiller, a semiretired plumber, was riding his red lawn mower back and forth across his lawn when we pulled up. He wore a white paper mask for his allergies. When he saw us, he cut the engine and pulled the white mask down off his face, so it hung like a weird necklace. "Hey there, hey there!" he shouted as he waved.

Jeff and I walked up the hill through the freshly cut grass and the clippings clung to our sneakers.

"Looking for some wheels, huh?" Mr. Dettweiller said to us.

"Like I said on the phone," I told him.

He led us around the side of his house, and when I saw the car parked in the driveway, I knew our search was over. It was a blue Buick Skylark, huge and square and ugly, the last of the gas-guzzler armada from the mid-eighties. The right front quarter panel was green and the hubcaps were mismatched. Frank said, "She's got a hundred and eighty thousand miles on her and the AC is busted. The radio only gets AM and the clutch is a bit finicky."

"I hope those aren't the good points," Jeff said.

I ran my hand along the side of the car, sensing her pride and strength. The front was a massive grille with a bumper big enough to sit on. This car was exactly what I needed, a battering ram on wheels.

Jeff popped the hood and began inspecting the engine. "Where'd this relic come from?"

Frank wiped the gathering sweat from his forehead. "She was my big brother's, lived down in Bethlehem. Damn cirrhosis finally caught up to him. She was sitting in his garage for years, and I've got no use for her. Runs pretty good."

"I'm sorry for your loss," Jeff said, and he and Frank exchanged solemn nods.

I opened the front door and settled in behind a steering wheel that looked swiped from a pirate ship. Jeff slammed the hood and shrugged, suggesting he'd seen nothing that concerned him. Frank gave me a thumbs-up and I reached for the single key in the ignition. The engine roared to life like an airplane's, and the seat beneath me rattled. The car felt alive, and eager.

Jeff, still acting like he was in charge, must have seen the shine in my eyes and asked Mr. Dettweiller what he wanted for it. The old man wiped the sweat from his brow, shrugged. "Say, eight hundred dollars."

Jeff didn't say anything. I just gripped the wheel and pictured the steep stretch of road that leads down to the Lookout over McGinley's Cove. Mr. Dettweiller said, "That price is negotiable, but she's a solid car."

Through the open window, I asked if we could take it out for a test drive. Before he could answer, Mr. Dettweiller sneezed and pulled a handkerchief from his pocket. While he wiped at his nose, Jeff said, "Before we could make an offer, we'd want Lute to take a look at it too, give it a once-over."

Given my intentions, it never occurred to me to have the car inspected. But I couldn't explain that to Jeff. Mr. Dettweiller came around and stuffed the hanky back in his pocket. He knelt down in the dirt, bringing his face level with mine. "Of course, of course. Whatever you guys need. Take her for a spin, get the old girl out on the road. No rush at all. Truth is, nobody else has even called about her."

"I appreciate the favor."

"It's no trouble, Anderson," he said. And here he reached through the window, patted me on the shoulder. "Anything for you and your family." I turned and looked into those red-rimmed eyes and I remembered seeing Mr. Dettweiller up at the UCP, squeezing his eyes tight in prayer.

Fifteen minutes later, I swung the Skylark into the parking lot of Victorio's and parked beside Jeff. "How's she ride?" he asked me when I got out.

I told him the truth. "That clutch is a bitch. But the brakes are good and she hugs the asphalt pretty tight, especially on the curves."

"Hard for something this big not to. That sucker's half tank. Probably gets three gallons to the mile."

I laughed and we headed inside. When we pushed through the double glass doors, a few heads turned and a sort of hush seemed to come over the place. Some people stared right at us. Just about everybody in town knew Jeff and I had once been a kind of couple. At the counter, Jeff ordered two plain slices. I got a Caesar salad. While they started on our food, we took a booth in the back. Jeff asked, "You want to run it by Lute's, see if he can't kick the tires?"

I noticed our table hadn't been wiped down and pinched some napkins from the mirrored dispenser. "I guess so."

"It's not worth eight hundred dollars."

"Mr. Dettweiller'll take six." The way the old man looked at me back in that driveway, I didn't doubt that he would take even less, but I didn't feel good about trading on Daniel's reputation.

"Probably so. Just be sure that it'll get from Lock Haven back to Paradise. Lots of steep hills between here and there."

The table was clean now, but I kept pushing the napkins around in slow circles. I wondered how far it was from Penn State to Lock Haven, if Jeff would like me to drive over and visit him some weekends. Then I caught myself and realized that my mind was slipping. I was indulging my own cover story, imagining the car beyond the next week. I was about to ask Jeff if I should take twelve credits or fifteen my first semester when a large figure came up beside our table. "Tell me something good," Gayle said.

From the grin on her face, I could tell she was pleased to have caught Jeff and me together. She held a white paper bag, and I knew she'd called ahead for lunch like she always did. I wondered what the grease stain on the bottom meant for her diet.

"What's happening?" Jeff asked.

"The usual this time of year. I'm already sick of Paradise Days and the damn thing didn't even start yet," she said. "College filling your head with radical ideas?"

He nodded. "Just like it's supposed to." He excused himself to go fetch our food.

After a brief silence, Gayle turned to me. "Daniel doing okay?"

"For now." I looked over at Jeff, who was behind a guy arguing about his order. "Did you hear this B.S. about Pilgrims down in the park?"

Gayle shifted the bag from one hand to the other. "I saw a bunch of out-of-towners heading into the woods the other day, up by the fairy fort. Albert Crawford told me some of them have come to be made whole."

"Made whole?"

"That's the term Albert says they're using."

I ripped my napkin in half without realizing I was tugging on it. "Any chance these Pilgrims came in with a wacko in a white bus?"

Gayle shook her head. "Bus belongs to Leonardo Castille. Went by the name Reverend Castle, the Fortress of Christ, when he ran the fire-and-brimstone circuit in western P.A. and Ohio long time back. In his prime, he was a certified Bible-thumper, but apparently he's mellowed with age. I thought I might track him down for an interview, but I'm swamped. You interested?"

Jeff returned, carrying a red tray.

"No," I told Gayle. "I'm steering clear of crazy people."

Gayle smiled. "Girl, you're in the wrong town for that."

Jeff laughed and set out our plates and drinks. "Come sit with us," he said to Gayle.

For a second, she and I looked at each other, then she said, "No, I've got to get back. I'm a bit shorthanded these days."

Jeff said it was good to see her, and Gayle turned to go. But then she stopped and looked back. "Take care of yourself, Andi."

"You too," I said. Then I stabbed a straw into my soda and looked away, not wanting to see her go.

Jeff said, "Something wrong with Gayle?"

I just started eating.

Jeff and I returned to Mr. Dettweiller's to tell him about the inspection Lute had done, which gave the car a relatively clean bill of health. Mr. Dettweiller shrugged and said, "So you interested?"

"Probably so," I told him. "But I need to sleep on it. Could I keep her till tomorrow?"

Jeff's head swung left and he stared at me. Eager to please, Mr. Dettweiller agreed and said he'd see me in the morning. "Take good care of her," he said, then swabbed his red, tearing eyes.

As Jeff and I walked back toward the cars, he said under his breath, "What do you need with that car overnight?"

"Nothing in particular," I said. "Just something I felt like doing."

Jeff stopped walking. "It's not much fun being lied to, you know?"

Of course, I hadn't been truthful with Jeff about a lot of things that day, so I couldn't blame him. But I also couldn't think of how to start explaining. We stood there without talking for a minute, then Jeff said, "Catch you later," and climbed into his car. He left me there in Mr. Dettweiller's driveway, feeling bad for lying to him and worse because I couldn't follow. But now that I had a likely vehicle for my Anti-Miracle Plan, I was ready to get to work on the other ingredient of my hoax: a pint or two of blood.

When I left Cohler's, holding a plastic bag sagging with supplies, I didn't head straight home. Instead I found myself cruising the lake on Roosevelt Road, pretending that the Skylark was mine and contemplating the places I could go. I found a decent country station on the AM and cranked the windows down, let the wind work through my hair. Over at the Abernathys', I saw my mother's truck and a dozen other vehicles, some with out-of-state plates. A small crowd had gathered under the Grandfather Elm. Since I didn't slow down, I couldn't say for sure how many I could or couldn't recognize, but that didn't mean they were Pilgrims.

I passed the country club, then crossed beneath the dam and turned north. Ten minutes later I slowed to navigate the hairpin curve over McGinley's Cove, then downshifted to encourage the Skylark up the steep incline that leads to the highest point in Paradise. At the apex I paused, but I couldn't do what I needed to do next in broad daylight. Besides, I didn't have a hacksaw.

I thought about driving all the way down into Roosevelt Park, confronting the black-booted Reverend Castle and the Pilgrims and whoever else wanted to make Daniel a small god. Maybe I'd even ask around about a thin, skinny guy with a perpetual itch. But I had a solid plan and I needed to stick to it. So I returned to the compound, knowing I could make good use of the time alone. I was pretty sure my mother would be home by dinner.

When I was a child, I remember being afraid of the toolshed. It sits off by itself in a corner of our property, leaning slightly under the weight of years. Pine needles cover the roof. It looks like a fine place for a witch to live, especially if you're a little girl. As I got older, my dad and I spent many hours in it as he taught me how to handle the tools, how to sharpen a mower blade and clean a paintbrush by spinning it in your hands. Together we built birdhouses and a swing for Daniel and even the Adirondack chairs on the front porch. Now I carried my plastic Cohler's bag to the shed, wondering for a moment what he'd think of my latest project.

Inside the shed, the naked lightbulb that hung from the ceiling was dead. I made do with the dingy sunlight forcing itself through the dirty windows, which barely reached the cobwebbed corners. I shuffled past the riding mower and the busted ten-speed bike, then cleared a space on my dad's worktable, shoving aside the mechanical guts of a leaf blower I'd taken apart but never reassembled. Before me, I laid out the contents from the bag: a tiny bottle of red dye, a couple cans of tomato paste, and barbecue sauce. For pure gross factor, I'd even bought a jar of raspberry jelly. From the rickety shelves behind the shovels and rakes, I dug out a box of dried blood that we used to ward skunks away from a strawberry garden that never took hold. Having no luck finding anything like a bowl, I dumped the rusty nails from a Folgers coffee can. Remarkably, it didn't leak when I poured in some water, and I began experimenting with different recipes, stirring my concoctions. Really, it seemed like I should be adding in lizards and bat wings.

My goal was peculiar: I needed a substance that, perhaps in the moonlight, might resemble human blood. At the same time, it had to be something that upon closer inspection (an emergency room?) would obviously be fake. This second part was especially crucial.

My first few attempts looked mostly like the guts of a strawberry pie, too lumpy and bright to be mistaken for blood. The second batch, heavy on the water and barbecue sauce, was far too runny. In addition, it smelled just like what it was. It wouldn't fool anybody for two seconds. Begrudgingly, I realized that cooking up my own fake blood wouldn't work, and I sat on the riding mower to review my other options. There was a bloodmobile that toured the area on an irregular schedule. Maybe I could sneak in there. Or St. Jude's — I was certain they had blood on hand. But this meant stealing, and more upsetting, taking away something somebody else might need.

My eyes fell on the veins in my forearms, and my mind turned to my own personal supply. Maybe the answer was storing my own blood until the time was right. What would I need? A syringe, one of those bags? The presence of my own blood would be a nice touch, I decided, a convincing piece of evidence in the midst of a grand hoax. But before I could pursue this course of action any further, I heard a truck door slam and knew I was alone no more.

As I walked up the hill from the toolshed, Daniel and my mother circled the Skylark. She asked, "Did you buy this?"

"Not yet," I told her.

Daniel climbed through the open window and crawled into the backseat. "It's gigantic in here," he shouted. "Like a cave."

"The car is awfully big," my mother said.

"Think of how safe I'll be in a wreck." I told her about Mr. Dettweiller and Lute Moody's inspection and she listened carefully.

"You know better than I do," she said. "I'll call Betty tomorrow and get the insurance straightened out."

"Thanks," I said. "I, uh, I appreciate it."

"I am your mother, Anderson. And I do want you to be happy."

Daniel was on his knees, bouncing on the springs in the backseat. He couldn't hear what we were saying. My mother's eyes looked sad, and I knew I'd been a topic of concerned conversation over at the Abernathys'. Or maybe she was wondering where this car could take me, my plans for leaving town. Whatever it was, she embraced me suddenly. I squeezed her back, and her chin rested on my shoulder. She whispered in my ear, "I love you, child."

And I said back, "I know that, I know." I hoped this might give her some comfort with what I knew was coming our way.

Long after midnight, I was back at my post in the Adirondack chair, waiting for my mother's bedroom light to go out. For as long as I could remember, she went to bed around eleven, disappearing into her latest paperback romance. Typically she passed out after a half hour or so, and more often than not she left the light on. When I lived up in the main house, I'd sneak in and turn it off for her so she'd sleep better. These days it stayed on till morning. But I couldn't be sure she was asleep now, and so I'd waited and watched and waited some more. Finally I realized that I was just stalling, and I stood up and headed for the Skylark.

The engine was even louder in the stillness of two a.m., and as I drove down the driveway I expected to see my mother in the rearview mirror, running out of the house in her nightgown. Maybe I was hoping she'd stop me. Roosevelt Road was empty, and every house was dark, as if the whole village were a ghost town. As I passed Jeff's house, I slowed and squinted through the forest, checking for a light or some sign of life. I remember feeling very alone. Chief Bundower was probably out there somewhere, gripped by his infamous insomnia, treeing raccoons with Pinkerton. He and I hadn't exchanged more than a dozen words since what happened at St. Jude's, but I know he didn't blame Daniel for his wife's death. I had to admit my mere presence on the road at that hour was suspicious, though, and if the Chief pulled me over and felt compelled to search the vehicle, he'd find the hacksaw under the front seat.

Turns out that the Skylark's left headlight was cockeyed bad. As a result, I had a better view of the shoulder than the middle of the road, something that made me feel slightly off balance as I drove. The approach to the cove from the north is a long, gradual rise, something like that first hill of a huge roller coaster. At the top, the part of the ride where it seems like the people in front of you are dropping into nothing, I stopped the car and cut the engine.

The world fell silent. Up on that summit, I'd reached the highest point in Paradise. From here I could see back to the town, south to the dam, across the lake to the open spaces of the country club's golf course. Most important, though, was the view right ahead of me. Roosevelt Road dipped down at a fierce angle for a hundred feet, the screaming part of the roller coaster ride, then hairpinned away from the lake. Right at the curve, there are a few guardrails, installed just after Michelle Kirkpatrick's prom-night disaster, followed by a flat grassy area where people used to park and admire the sailboats passing by the cove's mouth. The grass leads to a token wooden fence, just a series of interlocked railroad ties to mark the edge of the cliff. After that, it's a two-hundred-foot drop to the rocks.

With the Skylark positioned in the middle of the road, I shifted into neutral and stepped out. I steadied the steering wheel with my right hand at twelve o'clock and propped the door open with my left. The muscles in my legs strained as I shoved, and at first I thought the emergency brake was on. The Skylark didn't budge.

I put my back into it then, leaning my weight toward the decline. I faced the road and shoved so hard I thought my head would pop. But back behind me, I glimpsed the rear wheel as it slowly rotated. I felt a tightening in my back and my shoulders burned. I was at the edge of what I could do, but just like the wall you hit when you're running, if you push through it, there's always a hidden reserve of sweet golden fuel. The car moved an inch forward, then a foot. The front wheels reached the hill and the Skylark began to roll on her own, picking up speed so quick that I had to hop in before she took off without me. I had to fight the instinct to take the wheel, but this whole expedition was a test of alignment, so I forced my hands to stay on my lap. The car bounced and rattled, and every tree on the side of the road seemed like the one we'd strike. But the Skylark stayed straight and rocketed headlong toward the guardrails and the cliff beyond.

The wind whipped through the car and I felt a strange sense of exhilaration. My mind flashed to the terrible pressures that must have driven Michelle Kirkpatrick to suicide. For an instant, I thought of letting the car go, of riding it off into the open air, and the weightlessness I'd feel just before the plunge.

But that wasn't the plan for tonight, and my hands snapped up to steady the steering wheel as my foot finally stomped on the brake. The Skylark skidded and I fought with her to avoid fish-tailing. Her weight and speed were difficult to control, and the car came to rest sideways on the road in the middle of the hairpin curve, about ten feet shy of the guardrails.

The center guardrail was battered from cars taking the curve too fast, lined with streaks of every color of paint you could imagine. The whole thing wobbled like a loose tooth. I didn't think it would take too much for it to go, but I wanted to be sure, which is why I brought the hacksaw.

Between the guardrails and the drop-off, there's only about twenty feet, just enough space for couples to park their cars in the old days and look out over the lake. I drove the Skylark into that space and got out into grass grown tall as my knees. When I walked through, it shushed against my legs. I stepped over the wooden fence, crossed to the ledge, and peered down. Two hundred feet below, the lake water washed up against jagged rocks.

McGinley's Cove itself was empty, a fact which surprised me not at all. Nobody ever went in there. Rocks and the carcasses of smashed boats made the water impossible to navigate, plus there was no sand or even dirt along the shoreline, so what was the point? Besides, it was a well-established fact around Paradise that the cave at the foot of the cliff was a reliable place to encounter the ghost of Irene McGinley, or at least those of her drowned sons.

Worried that someone might come along, I went back to the Skylark and snatched the hacksaw from under the front seat. In the light cast by the half-moon, I knelt down by one of the gray posts that secure the guardrail to the ground. To test the saw, I set its teeth on the metal and began pulling back and forth. Tiny silver shavings drifted down like sawdust, and with only a few minutes of effort I had a four-inch cut. I set the saw in the grass and did some quick calculations in my head. The night of the hoax, the whole job would take about thirty minutes for all three posts of the center rail.

Somewhere behind me in the forest that stretches east for miles, something growled in the night. Not Pinkerton. Not a coyote. Something that sounded angry and lost.

Figuring that I'd used up all my good luck not being found out so far, I decided to play it safe when I returned to the compound. I parked the Skylark along the side of the road, fifty feet short of the driveway, and made my way in on foot. While I was tiptoeing past the main house, I heard a rustling sound from the back, like something small kicking up leaves. I imagined an early deer visiting the salt lick and snuck around the side. As I passed beneath my Adirondack chair, I saw my bat up on the porch. I grabbed it just in case.

After coming around the corner, I saw the clearing down below was empty. The rustling — nearby now — stopped. I wasn't alone. I held the bat with both hands and lifted the heavy end up into the air. Standing like a baseball player waiting for a pitch, I scanned the shadows along the back porch, making out the outline of the grill, the birdbath. Next to the air conditioner, there's an alcove where we store the garbage can. My dad and I installed a chicken wire gate years back to keep raccoons from marauding our trash. In the moonlight, I made out the glint of wire — the gate was swung back. "Crap," I muttered, relieved that all I had to deal with was some critter out for food. I lowered the bat.

Not wanting to corner a wild animal, I circled around so I stood off to the side, allowing it an easy escape to the forest. "Go on, git!" I said. "Ssst! Sssst!" Nothing came out. From five feet away, I peered in, but I still couldn't penetrate the darkness of the alcove. I didn't want to hurt whatever it was, but it was late and I was tired and a little ticked off. So I bent down and my fingers searched the ground for some projectile. They settled on a pinecone. Readying myself for something furry and small scurrying from the darkness, I sidearmed the pinecone into the alcove, maybe a little faster than I needed to.

"Not by your kind, liar girl!" the Scarecrow cried as he stepped out. Startled, I stumbled backward, tripped over a root or something, and found myself flat on my back. I reached around in the darkness, got hold of the bat, and scrambled up to my feet. In the shadows, Scarecrow hadn't moved. He clutched something hanging from his fingers, but I couldn't tell what it was.

I said, "Mister, I don't want to hurt you."

His free hand scratched at his shoulder. "You couldn't bring harm to me. The Lord shields me from my enemies."

Raising the bat, I said, "You sure you want to try that tonight?"

He chuckled. "I'll come to know your brother's heart. No matter your allegiance." He held whatever he'd taken from the trash in both hands. It looked like a dishrag but I couldn't see clearly in the darkness. "Even this fabric radiates with his aura, and I sense he has the gift. But I must be sure before I test him."

"How 'bout you just get the hell out of here and leave us alone?" I took a step closer, ready to take a swing.

But he didn't budge. "Your vile tongue betrays you, girl. I can smell your fear like stink. You don't confront me the least. For now I have all that I need."

Then he turned and hiked up the hill, back toward Roosevelt Road. He passed through a slice of moonlight and I saw for sure that whatever he took from the garbage was cloth, something dark and dirty. I mounted the rise and watched him disappear in the woods. Just like back at St. Jude's, I was glad to see him go. I was angry now that I hadn't taken the bat to his head, and I hollered, "Stay away from Daniel!"

Behind me, the front door opened, and I swung around to find my mother standing in sweatpants and a T-shirt. She snapped on the porch light and stepped out. "Annie? Who are you yelling at like that? What's going on?"

Keeping an eye on the forest, I moved to the porch. "That damn nutjob — the figment of my imagination — he was in our trash." I said it loud enough so that if he was hiding nearby he'd hear me. More quietly, I said, "He took something, a souvenir, I guess."

My mother rubbed at her eyes. "A souvenir of what?"

"Daniel," I said, and the moment I spoke his name, terror flooded my heart. For all I knew, Scarecrow had been in the house as well. Still gripping the bat, I shoved my mother out of the doorway and sprinted inside, took the stairs two at a time, and stormed down the hallway, past my old room to Daniel's. I shouldered the door but stopped dead in the dark. By the soft glow of a Superman night-light, I saw my brother's sleeping form. He was all tangled up in the sheets, and his head was where his feet should be, but I could hear his breathing.

My mother, who apparently had put together the threat to her son, appeared behind me. She settled a hand on my shoulder and whispered, "Thank the Lord Jesus."

We backed from the room slowly, and I eased the door shut. In the hallway, I turned to her and said, "First thing in the morning, we're calling Bundower."

"You're certain it wasn't just some lost hiker? A vagrant?" she asked.

"What's it gonna take for you to believe me?" I asked. "I recognized the son of a bitch."

I asked her if the front door was locked and she nodded. Then I stepped past her and went into Daniel's room, where I knew I'd lie on the floor awake till dawn. I kept the bat by my side.

CHAPTER EIGHT

The Chief rolled into the compound about nine that Tuesday morning, an hour and change after I called him. After a thorough inspection of Daniel's Lego spaceship, he carried the mug of black coffee my mother made him out onto the porch, where we followed while Daniel stayed inside, perfecting a weapons modification suggested by Bundower. The Chief blew over the steaming mug and looked toward his hulking car, a rounded black-and-white police cruiser that belonged in an antique car show. It was likely the only vehicle in Paradise older than my Skylark. From the backseat, his raccoon-chasing bloodhound, Pinkerton, stared at us, droopy-faced. The Chief asked me, "So you don't know this individual?"

I shook my head. "Not his name. But he was up at St. Jude's last week."

He and my mother traded glances. "You're absolutely certain of that?"

"One hundred percent," I said. "The dude is a psycho stalker."

"But you didn't observe him attempting to enter the house?"

"No," I conceded.

"And nothing was stolen?" he asked, looking over at my mother. She was wrapping a finger in the hair falling on her shoulder, an old nervous habit I hadn't seen in years.

"He took something," I insisted. "From the trash . . . Isn't that some kind of crime?"

Bundower turned to me before replying. "Probably. But mostly it's just plain nuts."

"Yeah," I said. "That's the thing."

"Andi," the Chief said, "if what you say about this guy is true, that he harassed you in the hospital and you had evidence that he trespassed once already, why didn't you call me?"

I looked down at the pine needles. "I didn't think you'd believe me." My mother sighed and rolled her eyes and I couldn't resist the dig. "That seems to be going around."

Bundower nodded and sipped, then wiped his mustache. Since his wife died, it had turned silvery white, bushy, and overgrown. It kept getting dunked in the coffee. He and my mother wandered around the side of the house, him leading the way and poking at the ground with the toe of his pointed boot. I sat on the swing and stewed. I couldn't tell if they were taking me seriously.

They were gone for a good ten minutes, longer than they needed to gather evidence from the mess by the garbage cans, which I hadn't disturbed. I wondered what they were talking about. In the months right after Mrs. Bundower died, my mother used to cook the Chief a meal every Monday afternoon. We always left it on his welcome mat, where the previous week's pot or Tupperware was always waiting, scrubbed spotless.

The two of them appeared from the other side of the house, and the Chief was tapping at every window as they passed. He set his empty coffee mug on the porch rail and considered me before speaking. "There's no indication of anyone trying to gain entry. I doubt you were in any physical danger."

"I can guarantee he sure was. That joker steps on our land again, and I'm likely to —"

"Andi, don't you go doing anything rash. This is a police matter."

"I'm not making any promises."

Bundower glanced at his watch. "Now listen. There's no reason to get all upset, but after you called this morning, I stopped by the park. Had a talk with some, well, campers of a sort, I guess I'd say. They're a tad on the odd side."

I asked, "Odd how?"

"Well, Anderson, just odd, that's all. Anyway, with your call and everything, I thought I'd drop by. They seem harmless enough. The mayor's taking it as a sign that Paradise Days will be a big success."

"Those folks aren't here for Paradise Days," I said. "They're here for Daniel." Bundower and my mother didn't look at each other, but that told me plenty. "You both know I'm right."

The Chief stepped forward and raised a hand to my shoulder. He looked me in the eyes and ran his other hand along his mustache. "I understand that you're worried about your brother. I respect that. But I'm telling you that nothing's going to happen to him. I'll post No Trespassing notices along the road before I leave, and I'll be sure Eddie drives by a few times on his shift. I gave your ma my cell number if there's any other trouble." There was an intensity, an honesty in his voice. And even though I didn't agree with him, I knew he believed that Daniel was safe.

He lifted his mug from the porch rail and handed it to my mother. "Thanks for the coffee, Nance." She reached for it with two hands and their fingers grazed when she took it from him.

As he strolled to his patrol car, he said, "All right, you two. Give a holler anytime, day or night. I don't sleep so much anyways."

My mother looked away but smiled when she said, "Thanks, Earl."

I figured he'd given her his number while they were inspecting the house. Bundower opened his door and spoke to me over the car roof. "And hey, you leave fighting the bad guys to me. That's what I get all the big bucks for."

I couldn't help but grin, and I said, "Sounds like a deal."

My mother and I watched him drive to the road and tack a few notices on some of the trees, then he drove off and we were alone once more.

The rest of the morning and the afternoon passed strangely. I stayed in the main house with my mother and Daniel, and a light rain kept us inside. He pulled out a box of dog-eared board games that we used to offer our guests, so dusted over it made us sneeze. Together, the three of us played Scrabble with all our tiles faceup, then kiddie poker with Monopoly money and a deck that we later discovered had no kings. While my mother made turkey sandwiches, I called Mr. Dettweiller and told him I'd buy the Skylark.

After lunch, my mother dug through the cupboards and unearthed a fondue set and melted some chocolate, and Daniel experimented with dipping everything from graham crackers to Oreos in the warm goo. Together we played Twenty Questions and cooked up a batch of iced tea. Daniel placed it on the rear porch to brew after the sun broke through the thinning storm clouds.

I couldn't shake the sense that the three of us were acting, pretending to be a family on vacation in this place. Now and then the phone would ring, but none of us moved to answer it, as if we were indeed just visitors. Maybe we thought it would shatter the spell if something from the outside intruded. Maybe we just wanted to stay safe in that little bubble for as long as we could.

Daniel wanted to make English muffin pizzas for dinner, so my mother headed in to Cohler's. Daniel and I lay on the floor in front of the couch and watched a cartoon movie about Japanese robot warriors. It was dumb and boring, but Daniel liked it, so I didn't mind. I guess the previous night's sleeplessness caught up with me, because I slipped away into a peaceful nap.

I woke to the sound of someone screaming in pain, and I sat bolt upright to find the robot warriors replaced by talking dinosaurs. But the yelling wasn't coming from the TV. I jumped up and ran to the kitchen, where Daniel was dunking Lego men in the chocolate fondue.

"What the hell are you doing?" I asked, shocking Daniel so hard he dropped the stick that the screaming Lego victim clung to.

"I was just playing," he said.

"You're making a mess. And scaring me half to death."

I spooned out the gooey men and put them in the sink, cranked on the water.

Daniel sulked over and helped me dry them with a dish towel. "I'm sorry," he said. "You fell asleep and the movie stopped."

I snapped off the water. "Forget it," I said. "Sorry I yelled at you."

I dumped the melted chocolate in the garbage, and Daniel asked, "Everybody thinks I'm special again, don't they?"

I thought about it for a second, then nodded. "Pretty much."

"Everybody except for you?" he asked. Put that way, it made me feel like crap, but before I could answer, he spun around, and my mother backed through the front door with her arms loaded with grocery bags. I hadn't even heard her pull in the driveway. Daniel turned back to me and I said, "Go help," and that was the end of our conversation. We carried the bags in one at a time while my mother unloaded. She'd bought Fritos and Yoo-hoo, treats we hadn't had in the house in years. While she put away the food, she avoided making eye contact with me, and I wondered what had taken her so long in town, but it wasn't something I could ask.

Before making the mini pizzas, my mother said that Daniel needed to get some fresh air and asked if I wanted to join them on a quick walk. I thought about the blood concoction down in the shed and told her I had to take care of a couple things. Yet when they walked off, I found myself just sitting on the front porch, watching the woods and thinking. Traffic passed by, far out on Roosevelt Road, and I tried to judge if the flow was heavier than normal. Now and then I thought a car slowed more than it needed to, perhaps, and I imagined the passengers saying, "There. That's the house where he lives."

When one of these vehicles actually took the turn into the driveway, it startled me good. But just as I was about to bolt inside to call Bundower, I recognized Gayle's Honda. It swung around the curves and pulled up on the gravel. Gayle climbed out, holding both her fleshy arms over her head. "I'm not trespassing, don't shoot!"

Gayle lumbered up the stone steps and lowered herself into one of the oversize Adirondacks. She handed me a copy of the new *Gazetteer,* the headline of which read PARADISE DAYS IS HERE AT LAST!

Gayle said, "It's on page six."

I flipped past the ads that I'd typeset myself and found the story. DANIEL ACTS AS UNUSUAL MIDWIFE. Gayle knew she didn't need to include his last name. Around Paradise, there was only one Daniel. There was Volpe's photograph of Daniel gazing at baby Miracle, which I recognized from the waiting room at St. Jude's. I wasn't thrilled by the article, but scanning through, I saw that it was really just a human-interest piece. There was no mention of the rumor of the baby being stillborn or any supernatural intervention. When I finished, I looked at Gayle, who was staring into the woods. She'd held back, told only part of the story, on my behalf. "Thanks," I said.

But she pretended she didn't know what I was talking about. "I figured you'd want a copy. More important, how's Jeff?"

I knew she'd deliberately changed the topic, and that was okay with me. "He's fine."

"He looked better than fine at Victorio's the other day."

"Quit," I said.

With one hand she played with the jangly bracelets on her other wrist. I could tell Gayle had more on her mind than the paper and Jeff. But I knew that unlike my mother or the Chief, Gayle would get to it. After a while, Gayle stopped fidgeting and asked, "So what's the latest on Daniel?"

The muscles tensed up in my shoulders and I didn't answer. Gayle saw my reaction and said, "I'm here as your friend, not a reporter."

I told her that Daniel and my mother were out on a walk,

then moved on to what mattered more. "That skinny freak was in our garbage last night, but Bundower came by and gave us the all clear."

Gayle's eyes widened. "I saw his little signs. Nothing like paper to ward off a lunatic."

"Better than nothing, I guess. He also told us there were some strange campers in town for Paradise Days."

"They ain't all campers," Gayle said. She took a deep breath and then exhaled. "Some are Pilgrims."

"Yeah," I said. "So I've heard. What do you know?"

"I know that some are down in the field and some are camped up in the fairy fort. People are claiming to have been healed. No resurrections or anything, mostly minor miracles. A lady with scoliosis says her spine straightened out. Some guy from Virginia swears his cataracts cleared up. He keeps pointing at things in the distance and saying, 'That's a pine tree. That's a bridge. That cloud is shaped like a bunny.' "

"Well, he sure doesn't sound crazy," I said.

"Crazy or not, Andi, people are coming. That's what I came to tell you. I've heard estimates that that service next Sunday will be attended by five hundred people, maybe more. Just this afternoon, I overheard the mayor saying that Daniel will be making a special appearance at Paradise Days."

"Daniel's going to Paradise Days over my dead body," I snapped. "And there's not going to be any service on Sunday."

Gayle turned and studied me. "What do you mean by that?"

Again I thought of taking Gayle into my confidence. I knew that if all went as planned and my hoax was a success, the *Gazetteer* would report the news to the entire community, broadcasting the fraud and forever casting shame on me and doubt on Daniel.

The sound of shuffling leaves turned both our heads, and around the corner of the house came Daniel himself, whipping one of the reeds that grows along the water's edge. My mother followed him, and when she saw Gayle she stopped and stared at me, wondering, I was sure, just what I'd learned about the world outside.

"Hey, Gayle," Daniel shouted.

"How was your hike?" Gayle asked. "Any sign of Samson?"

"Nope. But we did see a yellow-bellied sapsucker."

"Is that a fact? And what color was its belly?"

Daniel laughed and charged up. Gayle lifted the paper from the swing and unfolded it so he could see his photo. "Looks who's famous," she said.

Daniel frowned. "That doesn't look like me." He started sounding out the words of the headline.

I eyed my mother. "Run into anybody on your hike?" I asked. "Like maybe the mayor?"

My mother glanced in Gayle's direction. Slowly, because she had no place else to go, she ascended the stone steps.

I said, "You won't believe some of the crazy rumors Gayle's been hearing."

My mother steadied herself on the railing, but not because she was tired from their walk. "Daniel," she said, "why don't you run inside and get washed up? Then maybe you could bring Ms. Ehrlacher some of that iced tea."

"I should be going," Gayle said, leaning forward as if to rise.

"No. Stick around." I locked eyes with my mother, and Gayle

eased back in the Adirondack. I looked over my shoulder at Daniel, who stood silently with his hands at his side. "Go on, Little Man," I said. Sensing the tension, he took off inside.

My mother lowered herself onto the arm of one of the other Adirondacks, opposite Gayle. As soon as Daniel was out of earshot, my mother turned to her. "I understand that you and Ann are, well, very good friends, but I don't appreciate you interfering in my family's affairs. I can't allow that."

"Hold up," I said. "Telling me the truth is interfering? Mayor Wheeler's running around claiming Daniel's coming to Paradise Days. You make some kind of deal with him?"

My mother rubbed her hands. "There isn't a *deal*. Don't make it sound like some conspiracy. Mayor Wheeler ran into me at Cohler's and asked if we'd be going to the festival on opening day. I told him yes. We've never not gone. Why would we not go?"

"How about there's never been a bunch of nutsos camped out in the woods waiting for Daniel? How about no one's ever tried breaking into our home before?"

My mother looked up into the gray sky and exhaled. "Ann, the mayor's gotten calls from church groups as far west as Ohio. Tourists are coming into Paradise. Do you know how long it's been since that happened?"

"Tourists," I repeated. "So this is about money?"

My mother shook her head. "This is about moral obligation. Whether you want to accept it or not, your brother is blessed. And with blessings come responsibilities. These people are traveling a long way for something that matters deeply to them. And I'm not going to deny them that. Neither should you."

"That sounds just peachy. But what about Daniel? You forget your moral obligation as a mother?"

My mother's mouth opened in shock. She looked like she'd been slapped. Gayle said, "Andi, you shouldn't talk to your mother like that."

Gayle was right. Even then, in the heat of that moment, I knew it. Just like me, my mother always was doing what she thought was best.

"I'm growing accustomed to it," my mother said. "I don't know where all her anger comes from, but I know where it gets directed."

"Maybe this isn't my place," Gayle said, "but it seems to me that —"

Daniel backed onto the porch, bumping the door with his butt, carefully balancing a silver tray that held three tall glasses of brown iced tea and a bottle of Yoo-hoo. When he turned, I saw the smile he was forcing. I remembered how I used to stay awake with my parents, knowing they wouldn't fight in front of me. We each took a glass and sipped at the iced tea, and Gayle thanked Daniel and told him it was good. Daniel got a chocolate mustache from his drink, but none of us laughed. In that miserable stillness, all of us stared away from one another, and the only noise was the tinkling of ice against the shifting glasses.

And then another sound entered the quiet, a peaceful and melodious tune that at first you'd take for a bird announcing spring. After a few seconds, it was clear we all were drawn to the song, but it was Daniel who turned to the road and found its source. Raising one arm with a pointed finger, he said, "How come they're dressed like angels?"

Just past the edge of our property, on the shoulder of Roosevelt Road, stood six strangers, a choir clothed in white robes. I got to my feet and wondered where my bat was. My mother and Gayle stood, and we listened to the voices raised in song, drifting through the forest. *"Amazing Grace,"* the visitors sang, *"How sweet the sound."* The folds of their robes fluttered in the breeze.

"Pilgrims," Gayle said.

"They don't look like Pilgrims," Daniel said, no doubt imagining muskets and turkeys. "Are they out there singing because of me?"

I turned to my brother. His brown eyes were wide and nervous. I said, "No. They're just lost. Real, real lost." I started down the steps.

My mother followed me but had to move quickly to keep up. "What are you doing?"

I didn't answer, and behind me Gayle said, "Daniel, come stay with me."

"Ann?" my mother pressed.

"Just need to have a word," I said. "Help these lost souls get back to where they belong."

Even with all the anger pulsing in my blood as we walked the curves of the driveway, I could hear something pure in the voices of the strange choir. There was a girl my age, an old man with gray hair and skin the color of blackberries, and a bald guy in the middle of the bunch. They all beamed as they sang, radiating a peaceful, certain joy. Maybe because it was so far from what I was feeling, their faith only added to my fury. And at the time, my anger was all I was really aware of. I failed to recognize the rage of my envy.

The robed bodies of the Pilgrim choir formed a flowing white wall, and after me and my mother rounded that final bend, we stopped and faced them. From here, maybe twenty feet away, I could see that each one held a thin white candle, capped by a dancing flame. For just an instant I imagined they might be a gang of holy arsonists, come to burn down the compound. They finished "Amazing Grace" and rolled right into "What a Friend We Have in Jesus."

Despite my dirtiest looks, the smiles on their faces did not diminish. I turned to my mother and asked, "So these screwballs are some of the tourists we have a moral obligation to?"

Quietly she said, "Go on back to the cabin, Anderson. I'll talk with them, ask them to leave."

"Yeah," I said. "Be sure to point out the Chief's signs."

"They don't mean any harm."

"I don't especially care what they mean," I said. "They're scaring Daniel."

My mother stepped in front of me and grabbed my shoulders. "Well, you're scaring me. You think everyone's out to get your brother, that the whole world is against you. And somewhere along the line you've decided I'm against you too. Why? Just because I still hope things can get better here in Paradise?"

I stared past her, over her shoulder at the Pilgrims, as if I wasn't listening. But her words struck me like cast stones.

"Ann," she said, and the singing was gentle behind her. "When you were a baby, I'd find you in your crib humming to yourself. You used to carry leaves into the house to show me the patterns. Not counting the last few days, I can barely remember the last meal we shared. What did I do, Anderson? What did I do to make you hate me so?"

You let him leave, I wanted to say. *You could have stopped him.*

In her face I searched for the effortless understanding we once shared, before the ground swallowed my brother and the fish died and my father abandoned us. "I don't hate you," I said, knowing the words sounded hollow. And I wondered if I really did hate her, and if there was any sin worse than not returning your mother's love.

The singing stopped, and she turned to the silent Pilgrims. A big bald guy and that teenage girl stepped away from the group and started toward us, ignoring the No Trespassing signs. But as they neared, I realized that the bald guy wasn't simply bald. He was burned.

The skin of his head and most of his face was slippery smooth, melted by heat and flame. It was impossible to guess his age. The slick pink flesh extended over his forehead, where no eyebrows grew, and both his ears were scarred to unrecognizable nubs. The nostrils of the flattened nose were little more than slits. But under that, his mouth and chin, the skin glowed healthy. When he stopped, just a few feet in front of us, I looked at his mouth and it was perfect, the most perfect mouth I've ever seen. He had beautiful red lips, and when he smiled at us, his teeth were white and perfect too. The girl at his side spoke. "We know Daniel seeks no praise or rewards. We know Daniel is humble. We came to sing for him and offer our thanks."

My mother said something, but her words didn't get through to me. I couldn't take my eyes off the burned man's mouth. I wondered if he had ever kissed anyone with those lips. Shaking this thought from my head, I stepped forward. "You and your buddies need to clear off our land."

His perfect smile vanished, and the shine in his eyes dimmed.

My mother shook her head. "Ann."

"Like right now. You need to not come back here."

I could tell the girl was looking at me. She said, "You're his sister, aren't you?"

The burned man lifted one arm, and the robe spread out beneath it to form a white wing. He reached out and laid his hand on my shoulder, and even through my shirt I could feel that his hand was cool, which didn't make sense in the heat of that summer day. I turned my chin to his hand and saw the loose skin and the blue veins of an old man, but when he spoke his voice was clear and young. "Why deny the beauty of what you see?"

I recognized his voice as the one from the UCP. He'd been in there with Volpe while I was hiding under the pew. I looked down at his feet and saw the black hiking boots, then turned my face away and found myself staring toward the charred earth of Cabin Five. His voice was so sweet and full of hope. Part of me wanted to accept his words, but I held on to my anger and said, "Not everything is beautiful."

"And not everything is ugly," he answered, and he sounded so sure that I looked around again and fell right into his eyes, perfect blue marbles set in dead, tight skin the color of putty. I can't explain it, but something in his eyes made me think this man would understand, that here was someone I could tell everything to, all that I'd seen and felt: the flicker of flame as it engulfed a curtain, the heat pressing on my cheek in the snow, the fevered skin of my brother as he struggled to save Mrs. Bundower or pray the fish back to our lake. I thought this man could explain it all, tell me how I could have all this in my head and still be happy.

Reverend Castle smiled. "We will go now. I promise you we will not return to your home. I shall pray for your brother, Anderson Grant, and I shall pray for you."

Then the old preacher and the young girl turned and joined the other Pilgrims. Reverend Castle walked and they followed, south along the shoulder of Roosevelt Road, one behind the other in their flowing white robes. I felt a pull in my bones, the instinct to follow and find out where that burned man might lead me, but I let my anger rise up and I yelled after him, "Save it for the sheep!"

CHAPTER NINE

Wednesday morning I found myself once again wide awake and waiting for the sun to rise, though now I was in my old bed across the hall from my brother. Trying to think in the hours between midnight and dawn is one of the dumber things you can waste your time on. Every problem is either impossibly complicated or its solution is ridiculously simple. But with the morning light comes the recognition that neither extreme is accurate. Hard problems are hard, nothing more and nothing less. At night, you should sleep.

That particular evening, instead of resting and dreaming, my mind had been floating between the Anti-Miracle Plan, the day I had ahead of me, and Reverend Castle. I found myself oddly obsessed with his scars, and I played out endless scenarios imagining their origin. Perhaps he'd rushed into a burning orphanage or pulled a pregnant woman from a wreck wrapped in flames. Maybe he'd had acid splashed on him. The most far-fetched notion that occurred to me was that the wounds were self-inflicted. I'd read about monks who whipped themselves to show their obedience to God, and I wouldn't be surprised if someone like him would scar his flesh as a demonstration of his faith.

To be honest, though, this bizarre thought went against my general impression of him. Although we'd had just that brief encounter, there was a calmness that radiated off him, a deep ease I admired and envied. And then there were those strange, perfect lips and the melodious lilt of his voice. It had that deep hypnotic rhythm that you expect from most Bible-thumping preachers, but without the underlying hint of uncontrolled lunacy. He was a mystery to me, one I felt compelled to investigate.

But there wasn't much I could do at three a.m. The day ahead, I knew, would be an eventful one, with a trip to the bank and then to Stacy Wilbert's, the town's only notary public, where Mr. Dettweiller would meet me after lunch to do the paperwork for the Skylark. Since I'd already wasted another two hours on the blood concoction down in the shed after Reverend Castle and his choir left, I was contemplating a drive up to Scranton. Surely I could find one of those chain costume stores, one that might simply sell fake blood in the same aisle with the wigs and the pirate patches. Maybe I could track down Jeff and see if he wanted to come along for the ride.

Rolling around in my old bed, sleepy and anxious in the premorning's deep blue glow, I thought about Jeff, the two of us alone in the Skylark. Nothing could be more repulsive to me than being a damsel in distress, but when I was with him, I felt safer. I imagined him putting his arms around me, that big backseat, and my mind moved on its own in ways I couldn't stop. For a time, I found myself distracted from Anti-Miracle Plans.

When I finally did get up, I showered and brewed a quarter pot of coffee. All the things tumbling around my mind aligned for a second and I thought of an alternative to that long drive to Scranton. I remembered Scott Holchak in the school play at Paradise High. He was a wounded Civil War soldier returning home to his wife, played by Carrie Mulendez. When Carrie, who didn't even talk to Scott in the cafeteria, saw his bandaged face, she burst into tears. Seems like every year the school play called for Carrie to cry. That was her specialty. But Scott's bandaged face was the thing that interested me most.

It was just after seven when I climbed into the Skylark I would own before the day was done. I rumbled out of the compound without saying good morning to Daniel or my mother. Though I was pretty sure I had time to catch the football team, I didn't want to take any chances.

Paradise High School is on the west side of the lake, up behind the country club, so I had to pilot the Skylark south around the dam and then north again. In the year since I had graduated, I'd come back to visit with my track coach a couple times. And once Mr. Shulte called me over to help him fix the window unit air conditioner in the principal's office. Other than that, I'd avoided my high school, relieved that the experience was over and done. Now as I pulled into the parking lot, the brick building seemed smaller to me, tired even. I parked by the menagerie of hand-me-down cars and beat-up trucks in the west corner of the lot.

In the field just beyond, helmeted players jogged slowly around the perimeter. Everybody in town knew that Coach Breiner worked early morning football practices starting July first. He had the team meet him at school at sunup and they drilled hard till just before lunch. In baseball caps and white shorts, Coach Breiner and his assistants surveyed their men from folded-out beach chairs, complete with an umbrella to block the sun that hadn't yet begun to bake. Nobody even turned as I got out of my car and walked toward the school.

The door, left unlocked for the football players, led directly into the auditorium, an all-purpose room that served as basketball court, cafeteria, and theater. At the far end was a raised stage with a closed red curtain, tattered and dusty. Above it, a basketball backboard was pulled up tight to the ceiling, waiting for the new season to descend. This was the room I'd graduated in, the room where they'd held a memorial service for Michelle Kirkpatrick. To my left were stairs that led down into the girls' locker room, and to my right, the boys'. I marched toward center court, watched only by the scarred and empty wooden bleachers. Ahead of me, to the side of the stage, were the stairs you take to get to the weight room, and as I walked I can't deny that I was listening for some sound from below. Outside, I'd hurried in to avoid too much attention, and I hadn't taken the time to look for Jeff's van.

But the weight room was silent, no clank or crash of barbells that might signal the presence of my one-time kind-of boyfriend. So when I got to the stage, I did what I came to do and climbed up quickly. The red curtain was thick, like some huge sail, and I pushed it back and forth, trying to find the opening in the center so I could pass through. That's when I heard the voice behind me. "What the heck are you doing?"

I spun and there was Jeff, standing at the top of the stairs by the boys' locker room. My heart tripped, and not just from being startled. I didn't say anything, and he crossed the court and stood below me. "Little late for taking up a career as an actress, don't you think?"

Nervously, my hands kept sliding along the curtain, and one slipped through the two folds. From the far end of the court, I heard sounds outside the building. I extended my other hand to Jeff and said, "Come with me."

Without hesitating, he reached up and I heaved him onto the stage. Together, we snuck through the curtain and froze.

Out on the court, somebody said, "I'm sorry, Coach."

"That's why we tell you to drink orange juice," responded the older voice.

Jeff shrugged and we listened to the footsteps disappear into the boys' locker room. Behind the curtain there wasn't much light, and I could barely see Jeff's face when he whispered, "So what's the deal?"

Instead of answering, I reached for his hand. It was warm with sweat and calloused from lifting. I led him backstage, picking our way around stacks of tables and chairs, stowed here for the summer. We worked through the maze, leaving the stage proper and entering a cemetery of discarded props. There was a fake apple tree with a face on its trunk, a plywood wishing well and a unicorn made from papier-mâché. I didn't know what this year's production had been, but clearly it was some kind of fairy tale. This would be a marked departure from the Civil War musical they did my senior year, *Blue and Gray*. In addition to Carrie Mulendez's tears, the play had called for pretend guns, plastic swords wrapped in shiny aluminum foil, and lots of blood.

I opened the fuse box and found the master key that Mr. Shulte kept hidden there. Jeff seemed impressed and confused. He held up his open hands and hunched his shoulders to question what we were doing, but I held a single finger to my lips.

I unlocked the dressing room and let us in. Inside, I closed the door and flipped on the light. "We can talk now," I said.

Jeff scanned the room — a few dressing tables with tall mirrors, three racks of costumes, a couch from the sixties with one mismatched cushion. While I started rifling through the cosmetics in the drawers, Jeff stood over me. "I could help you look," he offered, "if I knew what we were here to steal."

I paused. "Something like blood," I finally said. And like that it was decided. Jeff would be an accomplice in my plan. I know that he's felt guilt over all that happened and wondered if he couldn't have stopped it that day. But he couldn't have. The notion had taken hold inside of me and was growing on its own by then. At the time, he didn't seem fazed by my odd response. Instead he sat at the table next to me and started shuffling through the fake eyelashes and brushes. We worked in silence, like cat burglars, and I didn't even hear him slip over to the metal cabinet beside the clothes. I was shaking my head at all the varieties of lipstick when Jeff said, "Bingo," and I looked over and saw him holding a thick tube with brownish red crud on the tip. It looked like caulk or paint. He'd already squeezed a little bit onto his hand.

I stood up and reached for it, but he held it behind his back. "I'll trade you the blood for the truth," he said. "You are seriously freaking me out and I want to know what's going on."

I knew I couldn't snatch it from him, but I didn't want to come clean, so I turned away and dropped onto the couch. A puff of dust rose up and I sneezed. "Sounds like a fair deal, I guess," I said. Jeff sat next to me and tossed the tube on my lap. I picked it up and turned it over in my hands, trying to decide where to start. Out in the gym we heard what I took at first to be thunder, but it was only the football players running the bleachers in their cleats. "That Pilgrim preacher," I finally said. "He came by the house yesterday."

"Came by for what?"

"He and his pals sang a couple songs. They wanted to see Daniel."

"Sounds certifiable to me."

"Maybe so," I said. "But there was something about him."

"Something like what?"

"I don't know. He just seemed peaceful, I guess. Maybe *holy* is a better word. I don't know."

Jeff picked at the armrest of the sofa. "I guess you heard about the healings."

"Gayle told me the latest. Next thing you know, folks will give Daniel credit for the sun rising in the morning." Jeff didn't laugh at my joke, didn't even smile. I bumped his elbow with mine. "What gives?"

"My dad quit drinking, Andi."

"Maybe the seventeenth time is the charm," I said.

Jeff shook his head. "This is different. He didn't make any announcements or grand promises. My mom just all of a sudden noticed yesterday. He's dry."

"That's great. I mean, I'm really glad for him. For you and your mom and all." I wasn't sure what to say. I didn't want to see Jeff disappointed again. Even back as far as sixth grade, when Mrs. Trent began talking about addiction in health class, everybody in the room made sure not to look at Jeff. The whole town knew Mr. Cedars "took to drink."

"I'm not saying it's Daniel," Jeff said. "But something's in the air. Maybe this is just giving people a chance to try again after they gave up. Maybe that's what a miracle is."

Jeff was looking me in the face now, and his hand was on my

leg. I turned away and pretended to read the instructions on the fake blood. "That preacher wasn't the only visitor we had yesterday," I said. And I told him about the Scarecrow rummaging through our garbage after midnight. "What's next?" I asked. "People breaking into our house? Me walking around with Daniel all the time like some bodyguard?"

Jeff shrugged. "Paradise Days'll be over next weekend."

"And you think this will end then? Weren't you here last time? We got letters from China. I heard the Pilgrim preacher and Volpe talking — they have some plan to take Daniel away."

"Take him away? Where'd you hear that?"

I couldn't tell Jeff that I'd been hiding under a pew with matches in my pocket. "Doesn't matter," I said. "I heard it."

Now Jeff stood with a huff. "You and your damn secrets. You wonder why folks keep their distance from you. I'm going to go work out. Catch you later."

Jeff had just swung the door open when I said, "Wait. The reason I know my dad won't help me. It's because I burned his cabin down the day he left us."

He swallowed once, studied my face to be sure I was serious, then said, "You burned it down?"

"Till it was ashes. I don't know why. He wasn't in it or anything. Maybe I just wanted him to know he couldn't come back. I'm not sure I've ever been so angry."

Jeff came back over to me on the couch and knelt down. He set his open palms on my knees. "One thing I figured out about you. The more angry you act, the more scared you are on the inside."

I believed what he said. "Guess that means I'm really scared now. I'm scared for Daniel, Jeff. That's why I need this blood."

Jeff slid up beside me, reached down, and took my hand. "Is there some part of you that thinks what you're saying makes sense?"

I took a deep breath, then began. "I think Daniel is in danger. I think sooner or later some nutjob is going to get to him. And if they don't hurt him, they'll scare him something terrible, scare him to the point where he won't ever be the same. Or it'll be like with Mrs. Bundower. These miracles will get bigger and bigger and before you know it, they'll have poor Daniel praying over a dying person. But this time he ain't three. He'll understand just what's going on. And he'll understand that he was supposed to save this person and didn't and he'll feel guilty for the rest of his life. Or through some fluke the person will live — that first time. But then more people will come or another preacher will pull into town. Don't you see? If this thing keeps on going, the only way it ends is with Daniel getting screwed up for life. I'm not going to let that happen."

Out in the gym the thunder stopped. Jeff was listening so intensely that I'm not sure he noticed. I could tell he cared, about all I was saying and about Daniel and about me. "I'm putting a stop to all this."

"How?" he asked.

"Kind of your idea, believe it or not. Yours and the Scarecrow's. I'm going to convince everyone that Daniel is a fraud." I held up the fake blood. "Saturday night, I'm going to send the Skylark over the cliff at McGinley's Cove. Then me and Daniel are going to climb down and I'll doctor us up with this stuff, make it look like we survived a crash no one could possibly survive. It will be absolute proof that Daniel's the

Miracle Boy they all want him to be. Sooner or later, somebody will discover the truth, and when it comes out, all the folks who believed will feel like fools. They'll feel tricked and betrayed, and they'll all leave Daniel alone forever."

Jeff processed all I was telling him, holding my hand lightly, now and then looking into my eyes, then away. Finally he spoke. "It won't work." For a moment I stiffened, ready to fight him on any point he brought up, but he continued, "The climb down into the cove is steep. It'll take you at least five minutes with Daniel. By that time, people will already be there. That crash is going to make a hell of a noise."

Jeff wasn't smiling when he said this, but something in his voice told me he had a solution. I knew that he was on my side, that I wasn't alone anymore against the world, and his face was close and I couldn't help but bring my lips to his. The last time we'd kissed was up in the fairy fort, the day that all this madness started. It had been years, but we fell right back into the old rhythm, and his arms came around my shoulders and we slid side by side onto that couch. When I got up to shut off the light, he knew I was coming back, and I knew we were in this together.

CHAPTER TEN

That night, while my mother and Daniel ate dinner up in the main house, I sat on the porch of my cabin to watch the sun fade from the evening sky. After my morning with Jeff, I'd spent the day in a kind of hazy shine, floating through the motions of buying the Skylark, taking a hike with Daniel, power-washing the back deck. Jeff and I hadn't discussed the Plan in much more detail, but having a partner in this made it seem more real, and once again, doubt about going through with it crept into my mind. Partly it was the pleasant buzz of my time with Jeff and the notion that life could be good. But all day long too, Reverend Castle's image haunted me. The last few sparkles of the disappearing sun winked out on the shimmering surface of the lake. Sometime after that, I glanced toward the house, where the dull blue light behind the living room windows told me Daniel and my mother had finished eating and turned to the TV. I wondered what they were watching.

When a set of headlights turned down off Roosevelt Road, I charged up the hill fast enough to meet the car before it reached the house. But it wasn't a Pilgrim or a journalist or Volpe come to try to steal my brother. It was Bundower in his bulky cruiser. He got out and closed the door, swatted at a mosquito. "Anderson," he said.

"What's wrong?" I asked.

"Nothing I know, especially. Your mom called and said she had some extra blueberry pie. I was in the neighborhood."

"Yeah," I said. "I know." When it was still light out, I'd seen him pass the compound twice in the same hour. "I appreciate that."

We shared a look and understood each other. I wanted to ask how long he might stick around, because with him here, I knew Daniel was safe. I saw his car was empty and asked, "Where's Pinkerton?"

"I only have him with me when I'm on duty," he said. His answer told me that he wouldn't be leaving any time soon.

"Enjoy the pie," I said, not especially caring about any other motivations he had for this visit.

When I returned to the water's edge, I crossed onto the dock and slid into the kayak. The moon was three-quarters full, and beneath its glow, I paddled north. The water seemed black, a color like midnight, and the lake was so calm that the emerging stars were reflected all around me. Now and then I'd stop paddling and just coast. I had the sensation that I was drifting through space, enveloped by darkness, guided by the distant constellations. I could've just taken the Skylark, but I liked the idea of approaching without being detected. The sleek and silent kayak seemed more appropriate for a spy mission.

I'm not really sure what exactly I expected to happen that night. I guess I just wanted to see for myself what I'd heard about from Chief Bundower and Gayle and Jeff. I wasn't seeking out Reverend Castle — at least, that's what I told myself. But slicing across that starlit lake, I kept imagining him ahead of me, like a magnet to which I was drawn.

As I neared the park, I heard the voices before I saw the flames. A breeze brought me smoke — rich and crisp. Up ahead on the beach, small blazes dotted the shoreline like signal fires. The flickering light illuminated the figures gathered in the shining, some sitting, some standing. The low, murmuring voices were punctuated now and then by laughter, a sound I found disturbing. I piloted the kayak toward land and drove it up onto the bank fifty yards south of the field, still safely hidden in the dark.

Soon I found myself in the same forest through which I'd run the night the Abernathy baby was born, though I avoided the trail and picked my way carefully through the trees and brambles. Nearer the park, the voices found me again, and again I saw those fires, now from behind. They were larger than I'd thought, bigger than you'd need for warmth against the night's slight chill. For a moment, I thought of the word *sacrifice* and wondered just what these Pilgrims were really up to.

But not all the people in Roosevelt Park that night were Pilgrims. Most of them weren't. Along the rim of the central field, a dozen or more merchant tents had sprung up like wild mushrooms. On the far side, the parking lot held RVs lined up like obedient caravan elephants. The first wave of Paradise Days profiteers had arrived two full days early. One industrious soul was already hard at work: A silver trailer hummed with electricity and yellow light, as a white-capped man greeted his guests with a smile, stretched an open hand for their money, and passed funnel cakes through a window.

Groups of people huddled on blankets spread across the great lawn, like survivors of a shipwreck floating on rafts, waiting to be saved. Beer bottles clanked. When I looked into the faces of those castaways, dimly lit by the bonfires along the beach, I imagined that they were watching their boat go down, doomed by an iceberg or snapped in two by some vengeful whale.

Twenty feet from me, a man wandered alone to the forest's edge. I crouched lower and looked away when he unzipped his pants and leaned back. He did his best impression of a dog at a fire hydrant. Under his breath, he mumbled a song. When he finished, he cleared his throat, zipped up, and staggered back to his friends.

As far as I could tell, nothing was really happening in the park. All these people were gathered here solely in anticipation of something yet to come. I wondered how many had come to Paradise to make money, and how many had come to witness the spectacle of Daniel.

This thought brought me back to my mission, and I squinted hard to try to pick out the white robes I'd hoped might lead me to the Pilgrims. But in the ten minutes I'd been watching, I hadn't seen even one. I knew they had to be there someplace. So I rose up and took a breath and stepped away from the secrecy offered by the woods, into the field.

No one paid me much attention. Lots of folks seemed to be wandering around, though all of them were in groups or couples. I seemed to be the only person walking alone. The few faces I looked into weren't locals, and I was careful to stay below the brim of my baseball cap. Gayle had told me that some of the Pilgrims were camped up by the fist-shaped rock, but the east end of the park was completely dark, no signs of life up there at all.

So I wandered ahead, the smell of funnel cake getting stronger and stronger as I neared the trailer. People passed me, ripping off chewy pieces of dough, fried and powdered white, and stuffing them into their eager mouths. I thought of how Daniel loved that treat, and how disappointed he'd be if we didn't come down to the festival. The year before, there'd been a thin old man with a beard that seemed stained yellow. He cupped spoons in his palms and clattered them together while he sang in a low moaning voice about life in the mountain woods. For weeks afterward, Daniel tried to imitate the trick, but his hands were too small.

I considered approaching the funnel cake vendor, asking him if he'd seen anyone in white robes, but the question seemed so absurd that I was afraid I'd sound silly. So I stood on the edge of the glow his lights emitted, and when the last person was served and left, he stared at me like an intruder. I turned away.

As I again crossed the field, faint music drifted up once more from the beach, not voices now but notes strummed on a guitar. Charmed, and with nowhere else to really go, I headed toward the water.

Embers floated from the flames and zigzagged into the starry night like fireflies. Shadows stretched out across the sand, almost reaching the field, but I kept far enough away that they didn't quite touch me. I walked along the edge of the beach, half listening for the guitar music. But all I caught were bits and pieces of conversations, something about how the government already had a patent for making corn into gas, something about the history of hemp, something about a renaissance festival with good sales in eastern Ohio. But no one was wearing white robes and nobody was talking about miracles or Daniel.

While I felt a little relieved by this, I admit I was also disappointed.

A breeze coming in off the lake cooled me enough that I regretted not bringing a long-sleeved shirt. Still, I had no interest in approaching one of the bonfires, entering a circle of people who'd want to know who I was, what I was doing there. I didn't really know what answer I'd give. The guitar music I'd heard was gone.

As I neared the woods where I'd stashed the kayak, I pictured myself paddling on the lake, not just back home but all the way to Cedars Marina, where perhaps I'd find Jeff out on the dock, just sitting and waiting. But then I noticed a smaller fire, away by itself, alone at the water's edge. The flames were dying down and, since there was no one near it, I figured it had been abandoned. I started for it with the plan of warming myself before getting back on the lake.

The crackling wood hissed and popped, and I stepped into its glow with my palms out. Just as the warmth reached me, I saw eyes through the flames. On the far side of the fire, with a guitar cradled on his lap, sat Reverend Castle. "Good evening," he said, completely unsurprised.

I froze.

He studied my face and clearly recognized me. "Why not sit," he offered, extending an open hand to a space right next to him.

Cautiously I circled the fire, then settled down, certain to leave a few feet between us. He looked at the sand between him and me and shrugged.

The fire felt good, and we looked into it together. The voices of the people by the other fires and out in the field faded. Behind me, the lake seemed to be holding its breath, listening and waiting. Finally I said, "So what, did you get kicked out of the Believers Club or something? How come you're down here all by yourself?"

Still looking into the fire, he said, "It seemed like a good place to sit. Besides, I'm hardly alone."

He said this the way you would explain a simple fact to a child, like the name of a bird or a tree. He let me think about his answer, then tilted over and offered his hand. "We haven't been properly introduced. My name is Leonardo. Everybody calls me Leo."

I looked into his putty face and nodded. "I'm Anderson." As I reached to shake, I saw that his fingers were fused together, making that hand more mitten than glove. I hesitated — he saw me pause — but then I slid my hand into his. His grip was firm but far from strong.

After we shook I said, "I didn't mean to — listen, I'm sorry that I —" I couldn't finish, so I shut up and let go.

Leo left his hand hanging in the open air. "Don't apologize. You still took it. That's more than a lot of people. If you'd like, take a look."

I thought it would be rude not to now, so I raised my eyes to his deformed hand. Along the tip of the mitten, two fingernails jutted from the melded flesh. They looked, honestly, like tiny claws, an observation I felt bad for even thinking. I wanted to know what had happened, of course, but I couldn't ask such a thing. Still, when he pulled his hand back he kept looking at me, and it was clear he was expecting me to make some comment. And before I could think it through or stop it, another equally rude question slipped out. "Does it still hurt?"

Leo's lips tightened, and he hugged his guitar to his chest. "Only sometimes. And not in the way you're thinking."

I didn't understand, but I nodded. "That's good," I said, which — looking back — was a pretty lame response.

I can't lie about it, there was something about Leo that just made you comfortable, even with how he looked and all. At that point in my life, if I came across someone who was handicapped, or disabled, or challenged, or whatever you're supposed to say this week, I'd just glance away. I wasn't being mean. I just didn't want to get caught staring and make them feel bad. Of course I've got a new perspective on all that now, but even back then, with Leo it was different. He simply radiated calmness. It was like the way I felt in church, before Mrs. Bundower, before Paradise Lake turned into a small Dead Sea, back when things were right and I thought God was there with us, hovering above and listening attentively. And strangely, being with Leo also reminded me of the sense I had with my father at times, the easy peace of working on a project together in silence.

We sat before the fire for a while without talking. Then Leo said, "This valley certainly is a magical place. Everywhere I look, there's beauty."

I'd never lived anywhere else, but I knew what he meant. "It's not bad," I said. I resisted the urge to tell him about the way the water used to shiver when the fish were feeding, back before they vanished.

He went on. "The mountains and the trees, the lake, there's so much to see. I grew up out west, and the land was flat, featureless really. Acres and acres you couldn't tell apart. Here, nothing's the same. Every view is unique. That's what I admire most."

At the mention of the West, I imagined Leo farming a field with a plow, a sudden thunderstorm, one bolt of white lightning, and a man aflame running through furrowed earth.

"I've never been west of Ohio," I said.

Leo said, "I'm truly sorry if we scared your brother. That wasn't what we wanted."

I knew this was the case, but I wasn't about to let him off the hook. In fact, once I recalled what I was doing there, I tried to generate some of the anger I thought I should be feeling. "One of your followers was ripping through our garbage the other night."

Leo adjusted the strings on his guitar and plucked out a note. He held a pick in the claw-mitten hand and worked the chords with his other, which was as perfect as his lips. "I have no followers. I don't lead anyone. And I promise you, none of the handful of people I came with would do such a thing."

"Well, obviously somebody would."

"Is that why you came here tonight? You came to find a trespasser?"

I thought about it and then shook my head. I hadn't been looking for the Scarecrow at all.

"Then why?"

I felt pressured, like I'd been called on in class and didn't know the answer. I scooped a handful of dirty sand and let it pour through my fingers. Without a good reply, I came back at him with, "Why don't you tell me why you're here? That's a question I've been wondering."

Leo played three rising notes. "I suppose that's fair." He repeated the notes slowly, over and over again, as if the answer were in the music somewhere. Then he stopped and gazed into the fire, giving his eyes a strange shine. "I came to Paradise for probably the same reason you came to this park tonight. I'm searching for something important. And I've got a feeling that some part of it is here. How's that?"

"What you're looking for," I said, "it isn't real."

"You sound certain."

"I am."

"That there is no God? Absolutes are dangerous things. They limit us."

I thought about his question. "Even if there is a divine being, He's not like we think. He's not sitting on a golden throne waiting to hear our needs and give us what we want."

Leo nodded. "Sylvia tells me that once you possessed a mighty faith."

"When I was a child, I acted as a child." I said this without realizing the irony.

But Leo called me out. "Strange for a cynic to go to the New Testament for support."

"I guess it's not all wrong."

Now he grinned. "Sylvia told me too about your theory on Moses, the plagues."

Volpe had come across a draft of that research paper on the *Gazetteer* computer and tried to convince me of the error of my ways. I told Leo, "That theory has some hard science behind it."

"No doubt. I've read the same studies you did. The volcano caused x, and x caused y, and y caused z. It all makes perfect logic. But what caused the volcano to erupt just then, precisely when God's chosen were crying out for help?"

I rolled my eyes. "Give me a break."

"I could show you something," he said, "if you'd like. Something that might change how you feel about all this."

I looked at him.

"Daniel's rock. Come with me. Up into the forest."

Of course, I knew the one he was talking about. "I've seen the rock before. I don't need to see it again."

"But you haven't seen what's happening there. It's extraordinary."

"And you think if I come with you, my faith will return? You think seeing is believing?"

He shook his ragged face. "More like believing is seeing."

His words felt like a magician's spell, and almost against my will, I found myself wanting to go with him. I wanted to see what Leo had to show me. And I was about to say yes, I really was. But accepting his invitation would have pulled me deeper into the thing I was determined to pull away from.

"Why can't you all just leave?" I asked. "Can't you find whatever you're looking for somewhere else?"

Leo smiled and his perfect teeth were bright even in the flickering half-light. "You've got fire in you, Anderson Grant. Medieval scholars believed that every person was controlled by one of the four essential elements of life: Earth, Wind, Water, and Fire. You, you're a Fire spirit for sure."

I didn't know what to say about that. What he said disturbed me, but I tried not to show it.

He went on. "That means you have great passion. You're capable of great love and great anger."

"Isn't everybody?"

Again, Leo grinned at my comeback. "Some more than others, I'd say. Tell me this — why does it bother you, that people have come here and feel good about this place?"

"They can come all they want, but leave Daniel out of it. That's all I'm saying. He should get to be a little boy, not put on display like some kind of circus freak."

I wanted the words back as soon as they left my mouth, knowing how hurtful they were. Leo didn't seem to notice the insult, but he was silent. Up behind us in the field, somebody had started to sing. Leo rocked side to side with the guitar. "I can feel your great love for your brother. It's as clear as the warmth from this fire. But so is your anger. I'm not sure where that's coming from."

I remembered what Jeff said about my being scared, but I kept that to myself. "Maybe I've got nutsophobia. I heard some of these folks are bathing in the lake."

Leo nodded. "I've seen them."

"But it's only lake water," I said. "It can't do anything."

"It can make them clean."

I couldn't tell if he was trying to be sarcastic or profound. "Okay," I said. "But do you think the water can perform miracles?"

Once again he paused before answering, plucking out those same three rising notes. "Only God can perform miracles. But people are weak, Anderson. Life beats them down and makes them forget what they knew as children, the joy and wonder of hope. Of discovery beyond their comprehension. Tragedy and misery find us all. Hearts harden and souls close like fists to the notion of God's grace. I believe that some things, things right here on earth, have the potential to make us reconsider the real possibility that God can touch us."

"And you've decided that my brother is one of these things?"

"I think he may well be. And for those who come to the conclusion that he is, I believe they need that hope like we need air to breathe and water to drink and warmth from fire to fight back the cold. You're young, Anderson. But you hardly seem naïve. Nobody gets through life without being wounded. I know you know what I mean. People can see my scars, but the fact is, I feel worse for those who are wounded inside. Outwardly, they may seem fine, but in their hearts they suffer from sin or loss or regret. Those that bear a secret pain bear that pain alone."

He stared at me then, stared into me, and the fire's touch on my cheek went from warm to hot. "I have to go," I said as I rose to my feet.

Leo stood too. "I know you're confused. I can sense your turmoil. Calm yourself and pray with me now. Let your heart be still and give God a chance to come back into your life."

I felt it then, the temptation to close my eyes and fold my hands and sink into prayer. But I pushed it away. "You really think that will help?"

"I can't guarantee anything. God decides these things, not me. But I would go this far — I'm sure that praying might help you."

"Might? That's a heck of a word to base your life on."

He shrugged. "Nothing wrong with 'might.' Nothing wrong with 'maybe.' At some point, I decided faith couldn't be proven. Faith is about believing more than what the evidence around you shows. Faith is accepting possibilities, not absolutes."

I looked into his ravaged face, those clear eyes so desperate to give me something. And sure, I felt tempted to drop to my knees and join him, but I knew I wouldn't. Not then. Still, he was giving me something important to him, sharing something he considered sacred, and I wanted to give him something back. "My mom is bringing Daniel to the festival on Friday."

He smiled. "Come with them. At least give yourself a chance."

I left his invitation unanswered and decided not to stick around. For one night, I'd been tempted enough. "Thanks for letting me share your fire."

Leo said, "Anderson, I can't read minds. I won't pretend to know you more than I do. But whatever it is, I know it still hurts."

I remembered my dad dragging those suitcases up the incline. But I clung to my rage and shook my head as if Leo Castille were a fool.

As I walked off into the darkness, I heard him speak behind me. "It doesn't have to be this way," he said. "Properly perceived, every wound can be a gift."

CHAPTER ELEVEN

On the Thursday before Paradise Days officially began, Gayle called just to check in and update me on the latest miraculous rumors: Harry Peterson's ulcer had stopped burning; a green sapling had sprung from the rotten sycamore stump in Misty Jennings' front yard; Daniel had been seen hovering over an Amtrak wreck in south Jersey. From the way she was mocking the Pilgrims, I knew how she'd react if I told her that I'd been awake all night, thinking of Leo and what he'd said, so I laughed along with her. After I hung up, I realized how desperately I wanted to tell somebody about meeting Leo. But when I'd called Jeff late the night before, his mom had answered and said he was tending to his father, who wasn't feeling very well. Plus I knew they all had to make final preparations for Paradise Days. So I kept my visit with Leo to myself, and I plotted out the finishing touches of the Anti-Miracle Plan in secret. Alone in the shed, I tested little bits of the stolen prop blood on my skin and my clothes. Though the stuff smelled awful, it dried a dark red that would fool anybody, at least for a little while.

About midmorning, I wandered up to the house and found Daniel on the front porch, playing Legos with that spaceship, apparently attacking a parking lot of Matchbox cars. I sat with him and tried to listen to his explanation of the epic battle, but my eyes kept turning to the traffic on Roosevelt Road. It was thicker than normal. In the flow of tractor trailers, RVs, vans, and cars, some vehicles slowed as they passed, kind of the way people do when they see an accident and can't help rubbernecking. Once or twice the snout of a camera poked out from a rolled-down window. I decided to take Daniel for a hike, mostly just to get him away from that road. So without even telling my mother, we took off on the trails. Together we searched for ancient arrowheads, chased lizards beneath mossy rocks, peeled birch bark and floated it on the lake, found mysterious indentations in the mud that we pretended were claw prints left behind by Samson the bear.

But when we returned home, we found something even more dangerous waiting for us. Mayor Wheeler and Sylvia Volpe sat on the porch, talking with my mother. I froze in my tracks and dropped a hand onto Daniel's shoulder, the same way I would've if we had come across a cougar on the trail. Wheeler and Volpe both looked startled, but they quickly turned their attention back to my mother, acted as if they didn't just want to stare at Daniel. I knew better.

Daniel charged up the stone steps, eager to show off the weathered turtle shell he'd discovered along the shoreline. The three of them listened to him intently, clearly abandoning whatever conversation they'd been having. My mother inspected the shell and wrinkled her nose at its muddy stench.

"Andi says we could clean it," Daniel explained.

"What'll you do with it then?" my mother asked.

Daniel shrugged. "I dunno. Make it a fort for Lego men? Why can't I keep it if I want to keep it?"

Volpe and Wheeler avoided eye contact with me as I leaned onto the railing at the bottom of the steps. By way of greeting I simply said, "Mayor, Ms. Volpe."

They both nodded in my general direction. Volpe said, "Congratulations on your new car."

"It's used," I said.

"New to you," the mayor offered.

My mother passed the shell to the mayor, who turned it over in his hands, then gave it to Volpe. My mother coughed once. "We were all just talking," she said. "About the festival."

Volpe bent to a knee next to Daniel, cradling the shell in her hands like a holy relic. "Do you know that it starts tomorrow?"

Daniel could hear the weird tone in their voices, and he looked down at me, still standing below the porch.

The mayor said, "There's going to be arts and crafts and games. Even a balloon ride."

I knew that they all expected me to be opposed to this, to start arguing with them like this was the worst idea ever. But I'd decided that a visit to Paradise Days wouldn't necessarily endanger the Anti-Miracle Plan. It might even help it. Besides, I wanted to see Leo again. I needed to see that rock.

So I smiled and said in my most cheerful voice, "Hey, Little Man, doesn't that sound like great fun?"

I thought Volpe was going to choke. My mother's eyebrows arched high on her forehead. Daniel beamed. "Heck, yeah. Are you gonna come?"

"Wouldn't miss it for the world," I said. I told Daniel to go into the laundry room and get the bottle of bleach, then meet me out back by the hose with the shell.

Once he was gone, the three of them regarded me suspiciously. The mayor said, "Your mother told us you'd expressed reservations about this. When did you decide it was a good idea?"

"I didn't. But you'd have brought him anyway. If you want me in on this, which you know would be better for Daniel, I've got one demand. And you're going to give it to me."

Volpe looked at my mother, and Wheeler crossed his arms, realizing that just about whatever I asked for now, they'd have to give me.

And so on the overcast Friday that Paradise Days officially began, Chief Bundower pulled down our driveway in his bulky squad car, our own official escort and bodyguard. The Chief's presence would keep any undesirables from getting too friendly, though I knew he might also draw extra attention to our little group. I kind of cringed when he brought the cruiser to a stop and boomed through the loudspeaker, "Your chariot awaits."

The three of us had been waiting for him together, and we went outside in a cloud of excitement and anxiety. The Chief got out of his car to politely open the front door for my mother, and I noticed his wild mustache had been trimmed neat. He let Daniel and me into the back, where the criminals would go if our town ever had any. An earthy scent radiated from the cushions, and strange smudges of sweat and mucus smeared the window's glass. Next to me, Daniel had a hard time figuring out the two pieces of the old-style seat belt. I turned to help, and found the mechanism stuffed with tufts of wispy gray hair I had to pinch free. I imagined Pinkerton pressing his wet nose against the window, eager to pick up a new scent and begin another chase.

A crisscrossing metal grate fenced off the backseat, and hanging across the front side was a rifle. I've never learned much about guns, and I wondered if it was a real one or just one that shot paintballs. Around town, some said Bundower kept that rifle just for show.

My mother turned around and looked at us through the metal grate. "All set?" she asked.

I finally got the buckle clean and strapped it across Daniel's lap. He looked around and said, "I'm supposed to have a booster seat."

From behind the steering wheel, Bundower eyed us in the rearview mirror. "That's all right," he said. "I know the local sheriff."

Daniel was thrilled. As we turned north on Roosevelt Road, he asked, "Can you make the sirens go?"

Bundower reflexively snapped a switch and blue lights strobed above us. The high cry of danger wailed so loud it made me a bit dizzy. Maybe following instinct, Bundower accelerated until he was going almost seventy around curves on the road that dipped and swayed like a roller coaster. Daniel whooped.

"Earl," my mother said. "Please."

The Chief slowed the car and reached for the dashboard. The sirens cut out, but the lights kept flashing. "Just trying to lighten the mood, Nancy. No need for everybody to be so tense. Look here now. This is going to go smooth and easy."

When we got to the parking lot, Bundower waved at Lute Moody instead of giving him the five dollars he held a hand out for. The Chief maneuvered the cruiser up through some RVs and other cars, finally finding a spot near Leo's funky white school bus. Faded blue spray paint on the side declared, PROUD TO BE A JESUS FREAK!

My mother got out on her own but the Chief had to open the door for Daniel and me. A few tourists passed by and seemed curious, but I had the feeling it was because a family emerging from a police car just looks strange, not because anybody recognized Daniel. My mother took his hand and they scooted ahead, toward the gap in the forest that leads to the field.

"Okay," I said to Bundower, alone with him for the first time. "So what's gonna be our secret signal?"

"Secret signal?"

"Right. Have we got a code or something in case there's trouble?" I was only half kidding, but now that we were there, I didn't know what to expect from the Pilgrims.

"Sure," Bundower said, "the secret code. You shout my name as loud as you can. Sound good?"

He fanned his fingers across his pistol, which as far as I knew had never come out of its holster, let alone been fired. I wondered if he even had bullets. But there was a little iron in the Chief's voice that I hadn't heard before, and I nodded. "Nancy," he hollered, "don't go getting too far ahead."

My mother slowed and we joined them. I took Daniel's other hand, and Bundower led the way. We mixed in with the crowd of tourists funneling through the entrance, beneath the same ratty banner I'd run under the night of the Abernathy baby's birth. The colors seemed even more faded, and the CELEBRATE PARADISE DAYS! struck me as mostly a stupid joke.

We crossed through the forest, only a thin patch at that spot, and stepped into the field, where the festival spread out before us.

"Whoa!" Daniel shouted, startled by the hot air balloon, bright red and suspended in the dull gray sky. It hung in the middle of the park like the centerpiece on a dining room table. From a hundred feet up, two people I didn't recognize waved down at the crowd.

"Can we go in the balloon?" Daniel wanted to know.

"No," my mother answered. "That's not a ride for kids."

"Let the boy have some fun, Nancy," Bundower said over his shoulder.

"We'll see," my mother said, glaring at the back of the Chief's head.

I imagined being in the balloon with Daniel. We'd float over the lake and over the mountains and drift east, toward the Atlantic. I pictured us coming down in a faraway land with sand dunes and camels, where they'd never heard of Paradise or the Miracle Boy who was saved from certain death.

It was just after noon, and the festival wasn't nearly as packed as I'd expected. Scattered across the huge field were a few hundred people, give or take. Most of the thin crowd flowed to our right, up a long alley of booths, merchant tents, and boxy concession trailers. Below us, on the beach, a couple kids tossed a Frisbee, and somebody was flying a Chinese dragon kite. I also caught sight of a dozen Jet Skis beached in the sand. I didn't see Jeff or his dad.

"So which way?" Bundower asked.

My mother shrugged and looked at me.

Jeff was likely along the beach, but above us was the forest and the rock, probably Leo. "Let's do the loop," I said, knowing that the alley of vendors curved around the rim of the entire field. It would bring us around to the beach eventually.

So off we went, the four of us walking along like anybody else. We passed a black tent where a man with a huge beard lined his table with leather belts, leather purses, leather wallets, even leather Bible covers with the words LIFE'S INSTRUCTION MANUAL branded on the front. Bundower held up a black leather hat and raised his eyebrows at me, but I told him I was fine with my baseball cap. We passed a sizzling metal cart with a guy frying Twinkies and Snickers and Oreos. Farther up, a middle-aged couple — maybe man and wife, maybe brother and sister — were selling swings crafted from recycled rubber tires. Kids were crawling all over a shiny new medical helicopter from St. Jude's on display by a fire engine. Some were flat on the ground nearby, pretending to be mortally wounded.

I'm not sure if I'd just expected everybody to stop what they were doing and stare at Daniel or what, but nobody seemed to be noticing us all that much. As we zigzagged up the alley, I found myself hoping that maybe all the stories had been simply blown out of proportion. Maybe there were only a handful of Pilgrims and they were like Leo, kind and harmless. Sure, a few people nodded and smiled at Daniel, but these were locals from town just being friendly. As a whole, the crowd seemed a lot more interested in buying corn dogs and tie-dyed T-shirts.

My mother pulled us into the back of a group watching a man with a chain saw carving away at a wooden stump. He'd touch the spinning teeth to the block and sawdust would spit out. Tiny shreds flecked his red beard, and the red hair on his arms was coated with fine dust. I thought at first he was making an eagle. The wings were pretty clear. Daniel couldn't see, so Bundower hoisted him up on his shoulders. When the man paused from his work to wipe the sweat from his forehead, the chain saw fell silent and Daniel said, "That's gonna be a angel."

The lumberjack artist smiled at Daniel and gave a thumbs-up. A few in the crowd turned to us and it occurred to me that anybody from outside Paradise might mistake the four of us for a family, just a mother and father and two kids out for a day at the local festival.

Up near the picnic pavilions, an area was set off for the "Garden of Eden" bobbing-for-forbidden-apples contest, a corny contest to have in a place called Paradise. At the horseshoe pit, the competitors were practicing. Three-time champ Thurman Griggs lofted a horseshoe in a soft arc and it rotated slowly, floating above the heads of the spectators before dropping from my sight. Metal clanked on metal. The warm smell of Jennifer Newman's peach cobbler lured people into her tent, licking their lips. Beneath a makeshift sign that read PARADISE PIES, she was selling slices for a dollar and whole pies for five. My mother turned to Daniel and asked, "Cobbler now or wait for funnel cake?"

From Bundower's shoulders, he said, "Cake."

We paused at a booth with a guy trying to sell stones shaped like famous people. My mother liked the one of George Washington, but Bundower said it looked like Bob Hope. Daniel lingered by a face painter working a brush over the cheeks of a five-year-old, who was either a scary clown or a goofy-looking lion.

We hiked up the incline a bit farther, and Daniel, riding again on Bundower's shoulders, pointed a finger toward a tent beneath the shade of a sprawling maple. Inside, a woman made wax candles in the shapes of dragons and wizards. She wore a red cone hat with white stars on it, as if she were a sorceress. Her hands warmed a piece of wax over a tender blue flame and her fingers pushed and twisted, shaping. Bundower put Daniel down and lifted up a wax damsel who resembled Sleeping Beauty. Daniel held a rounded green knight wielding a sword straight over his head. A wick poked from the tip of his blade. Daniel turned to my mother and said, "I'd never ever light it."

My mother started talking about the hazards of a fire, but Bundower gave her a look and she reached into her purse. The sorceress woman carefully wrapped the knight in butcher paper before stashing it in a plastic bag.

Finally we reached the top of the field, the eastern edge that runs up against the forest. Like they did every year, they had constructed a large wooden bandstand for the musical acts that would perform later in the afternoon and evening, and it was strategically placed to cover the clear-cut path the rescuers had chainsawed the night Daniel was in the well. A bunch of people sat on the edge of the empty stage, looking down over the field. Bundower boosted Daniel up, and I sat next to him. My mother walked over to get in line for funnel cake. Below us, the red balloon had again touched down and was loading up more passengers. Beyond that, a neon-green Jet Ski buzzed along the lake. I squinted to see if Jeff was riding it, but from that distance I couldn't tell.

"Look here," Bundower said to me. "I'm not sure what the mayor had in mind, but seems like nobody cares we're here."

"Fine by me," I said.

Daniel unwrapped his knight and rolled it in his hands. His swinging heels knocked against the wood. I told him to be careful not to break the wax sword off.

I pictured myself standing up on the stage and addressing

the crowd, holding a megaphone and announcing, "Come see the amazing Miracle Boy!" If people were willing to pay to have their faces badly painted, and for fried Twinkies and rocks shaped like E.T., what price would they pay to be healed? If Daniel were the real thing, if he could actually take away pain and suffering, if Leo was right and my brother could help lift regret, who wouldn't want it? Everyone in Paradise would line up. Everyone in the world.

"Can I go play?" Daniel asked me. He was looking at the rear of the stage, where a few kids were circling each other.

"The candle stays," I said.

He frowned but handed it over, and then joined the other children. I watched them for a minute, then turned back and stared at the crowd. I thought about what Leo said about everyone having wounds, and as each person passed, I'd look into his or her eyes and wonder, *What healing do you need?*

Bundower, who'd been standing guard on the edge of the stage, wandered closer to me and stood with his thumbs shoved into his gun belt. "You might not give your ma such a hard time."

I kept watching the crowd. "What's the secret signal for my wanting advice on how to deal with my mother?"

"She's been through a good bit. You could cut her some slack."

"What's it to you?"

"I'm just saying. She's your mother. Wouldn't cost you anything to show the lady some respect."

My mother returned carrying paper plates loaded with funnel cake and a couple cans of Coke. "Daniel," I shouted over my shoulder, "lunch."

My mother said, "Guess who I found?" and when I looked back, Volpe and Wheeler were following her.

Volpe smiled widely, but the mayor frowned at Bundower. "I thought we agreed you'd notify me when you arrived."

"Cool your jets," Bundower said. "You haven't missed any photo opportunities."

Volpe stood before me. Even in the gray light, her gold glasses shone. "How are you, Anderson?"

"I'm perfect," I said. "Even better now that you're here."

Daniel sat again next to me, and my mother gave us one of the funnel cakes, which I put on my lap. The heat seeped through the paper plate and warmed my leg. My mother offered some of hers to Bundower, and he peeled free a piece of the fried dough, dipped it in the sugary powder, and took a bite.

The mayor studied the sky. "I'm sure the sun's going to burn through this."

Volpe said to Daniel, "What's that you have?" and she lifted it from the stage. Carefully, she examined the candle. "King Arthur and his Round Table had a sacred quest. The search for the Holy Grail."

I rolled my eyes. Funnel cake makes you thirsty — sticks to the roof of your mouth. I didn't mind sharing a Coke with Daniel, but I wasn't sure how I felt about my mother and Bundower passing one back and forth.

Volpe told Daniel, "The Holy Grail was Jesus' chalice, and it was said to have wondrous powers."

"When you're finished eating, maybe we should walk around more," the mayor said to my mother. "Give everyone a chance to see that Daniel's here."

"We could just float him up in the balloon and make an announcement," I suggested.

My mother shook her head and sighed, "Ann."

Bundower shot me a look, and I said, "Sorry," then took a bite of funnel cake. My mother seemed surprised by my apology.

"What's a chalice?" Daniel asked.

Before I could answer, from around the side of the stage came a familiar voice. "It's a kind of special cup."

We all turned and there was Leo, wearing jeans and a clean white T-shirt. Behind him on either side were two other men, both from the choir I'd chased off. "Hello, Anderson," Leo said.

Everybody — the Chief and my mother and Volpe and the mayor — snapped their faces to me, shocked that he knew my name. I nodded. "Hey, Leo."

In turn, Leo greeted everyone. He was very polite and proper.

Nobody shook hands or anything, but the introduction felt very formal, like we'd been sent by our tribes to arrange a truce. Daniel and me slid down off the stage, and all of us kind of stood there a bit stunned. We'd all been anticipating this moment, but none of us knew quite what to do now that it was here. At first people just walked past, but then a few stopped. Maybe they recognized the mayor, or maybe they noticed Leo's burns, or maybe they just sensed the tension in the silence between our two groups. In no time at all, a small crowd had formed, and the people began whispering back and forth. And now the out-of-towners were taking a hard look at Daniel, and I think some of them were figuring out just why that little boy looked so familiar.

It was Daniel who broke the standoff. He reached up on the stage for the paper plate. Without explaining or asking permission, he walked past my mother and Bundower, crossed the open space between us and the Pilgrims, and stepped right up to Leo. He held the plate up and said, "You like funnel cake?"

Leo smiled with those perfect teeth. "I've never tried it, to be honest."

"You got to rip it."

Leo reached down and tore a chunk. All eyes were on him as he ate, as if it were some grandly symbolic act. He licked his lips. "It's good."

"You can have the rest," Daniel said. "We got more."

Leo held up a hand, like he was about to say no, but then he reconsidered and took the plate from Daniel. "Thank you."

Daniel said, "You're welcome," and returned to the stage. I stood behind Daniel and put my hands on his shoulders.

Bundower lifted his chin at Leo. "Look here. Where are all your pals?"

"There are others nearby," Leo said. "They're waiting."

"Waiting for what?" one of the onlookers asked.

And none of us, not the Pilgrims nor me nor my mother, could keep from giving away the answer. We all turned to Daniel. He blinked and smiled, then slid behind me and wrapped one arm around my leg.

Leo looked me in the eye and said, "We didn't want to overwhelm him. I asked them to be patient."

"So you are their leader," I said.

He shook his head. "Most of them I'd never met before coming to this place. But they seem to respect my opinion."

The crowd around us was growing larger. Still holding Daniel's knight, Volpe stepped forward. "Many have traveled far to see him," she said to me.

"That's true," Leo said. "Consider how many more could not make the journey."

The two guys with Leo both nodded their heads at this, and I wondered what it meant.

Leo bent down, bringing himself eye to eye with Daniel. "There is something I'd like very much for you to see."

"The rock," I said. "Up in the fairy fort."

Leo nodded. "Yes. The rock. That's where everyone's gathered."

"What's up there?" my mother asked.

Volpe said, "It's the sort of thing you must see for yourself."

The mayor stared at Volpe. "Sylvia, you've been up there already?"

"Oh, yes," she said and her voice was light and dreamy. "It's wonderful."

Bundower put his back to Leo, faced me and my mother. "This is totally your call."

My mother rubbed her hands, opened her mouth, closed it, and looked absently in my direction. Daniel said, "I want to see something wonderful."

I shrugged, trying to act like I didn't care. "I guess it's why we came."

"No use waiting then," Bundower said. And with that he scooped Daniel up onto his shoulders and turned to Leo. "Lead the way."

CHAPTER TWELVE

Looking back, I know now that I underestimated the strength of the Pilgrims' faith. Or their need. Or their dreams, maybe. Or whatever it is that you want to call the belief that life can be better than what it is. That's what lured them all to Paradise, the ones who came with Leo and the ones who came on their own. That belief fueled their desire to see Daniel as miraculous. From where I am now, of course, it's easy to see. But when I was in the middle of it, I was too focused on what was right in front of me. I couldn't see the big picture. It's the difference between the view from the valley and the view from the mountaintop.

So imagine Leo guiding our little group up the trail into the forest. And a crowd of festivalgoers, mostly people from outside Paradise, following us along that twisting path, which was marked by stumps from the midnight clear-cut. Nobody talked, so as the noises from Paradise Days lessened and then vanished, the only sound was feet kicking leaves, and squirrels scrambling in the branches overhead. From the Chief's shoulders, Daniel was tallest among us. He must've realized where we were going, but I couldn't get a read on how he felt about that. As far as I knew, he'd never been back to that place in all the years since his accident.

In a way, it felt like we were walking back through history. Less than a minute after leaving behind the modern world, we passed the low stone walls stacked by Colonial farmers to mark off their property, back when that part of the forest was still open field. Of course, the night Daniel was in the hole the men plowed right over the wall that was in their way, and afterward no one went back to repair the tumbled rock. Deeper in, we cut through the orchard of wild apple trees, descendants of some distant farmer. Untended for generations, and deprived now of full sunlight, the misshapen trees grew twisted and close to the ground. On one of our long-ago hikes, Jeff and I plucked green apples from the gnarled limbs. Legend had it that the fruit was poisoned, but really it was just bitter.

And then at last we climbed the rise that overlooks the fairy fort, so old no one even pretends to guess its origin. My mother and Mayor Wheeler were leading the way with Leo and Volpe, so they were the first to see, and the sight down in the crater stopped them dead in their tracks. My mother gasped and covered her mouth. At her side, Volpe said, "Blessed be Jesus."

Bundower and I stepped up, and the scene spread out before us. Below, in the ancient and scattered circle of stones, maybe a hundred Pilgrims waited, facing us. All perfectly silent, like some garden of statues. Some held hands, but most stood alone. All their faces lifted toward Daniel with what I can only describe as a brightness. Imagine on a winter day, when the sun breaks through the clouds and you turn to face the warmth. That's how they were looking at my brother.

This would be easier if I could describe the Pilgrims as just young or old, or rich or poor, crazy-looking or sane, but there were all kinds. There were babies being held and toddlers clinging to their parents, teenagers and businessmen, a woman in patched blue jeans thrusting a tattered Bible over her head, a frail, gray-bearded farmer in overalls, puffing on a pipe. From outward appearance, they had nothing in common except for the fact that they had gathered here in this place. A dozen tents had popped up in between the rocks, some worn and ragged, some still shiny with their newness.

At the center of the congregation, the very heart of the fairy fort, sat the fist-shaped rock, surrounded by what I took at first for a heap of trash.

From the rise, Leo lifted an open palm in greeting to the Pilgrims below. "I told you he would come."

The Pilgrims exchanged smiles, thrilled and anxious. A few clapped and someone shouted out, "Praise the living God." Leo started to descend, picking his way carefully down the inside slope, and we followed. Daniel wrapped his arms around the Chief's head and the Chief took hold of Daniel's ankles. The crowd of maybe a few dozen festivalgoers who'd come with us that far didn't join us down in the fairy fort. Instead they spread out along the rim of the crater, not too sure of what was going on, but certain they wanted a good view for whatever was coming.

Leo led us around the rocks and through the scattered congregation. Walking next to me, Bundower tapped on Daniel's leg. "How you doing up there?"

"Who are all these people?" Daniel asked as we passed through them.

Those who were close enough to hear, including Volpe and the mayor just ahead of us, laughed at the question. The sound radiated out from us as others chuckled as well, and this bothered me. I'd forgotten that the shape of the fort magnified sound, and it seemed like even the forest above us was laughing.

Leaning in close to me, Bundower whispered, "Look here. You make out that guy from your backyard, you point him out."

I nodded. "You'll be the first to know."

Bundower raised his voice. "Nancy," he said, "you okay with where we are with this?"

From between Volpe and Leo, my mother glanced back and said she was just fine. She had that look like she did the night she drove Daniel to the Abernathys' — nervous but determined — like she was being tugged in a direction she wasn't quite sure she wanted to go. I knew how she felt.

Working our way closer to the center, we passed pilgrims who bowed and some who knelt. All backed away from our path. Those who didn't avert their eyes out of awe or respect gazed up at Daniel like he was some minor deity.

Just ahead of us, my mother said, "I don't understand," and I saw the stuff that from the rim I'd mistaken for garbage. Backed against the fist-shaped rock was an electric wheelchair, the deluxe scooter kind with three knobby tires and a stick for a steering wheel. Seated on the cushioned chair, as if it were a kind of holy throne, was a golden-framed photograph of Daniel. It was his bloodied and swollen face from a magazine cover, blown up to many times its original size.

From the Chief's shoulders, my brother pointed and said, "Hey, Andi. That's me."

The Pilgrims seemed pleased.

Piled against the wheelchair, abandoned medical gear mixed with strange curiosities. Three wooden canes crossed over drenched and crumbled packages of Marlboro cigarettes. A full bottle of whiskey tilted against a battered green oxygen tank. An asthma inhaler capped a pyramid of brown pill bottles. Hypodermic needles encased in plastic were scattered across a ripped-up fur coat. Sharp fragments of sliced-up credit cards littered the ground near a suitcase that looked brand-new. A pool cue rose from the heap like the skinny mast of a ship. An X-ray film of a spine patched with bolts and screws lay nestled inside the white shell of an orthopedic back brace.

My mother squatted down to a filthy car seat that held a milk carton showing the black-and-white image of a missing child. When she remained quiet, Mayor Wheeler asked the obvious question. "Can somebody tell me what I'm looking at?"

Leo pulled free a single aluminum crutch from the pile and held it, smiling. "Proof," he said. "Evidence left behind by those who've felt the healing."

A satisfied murmur rolled through the Pilgrims. Many nodded and someone shouted, "Amen!" Slowly, they were creeping nearer, gathering around us.

Leo continued, "And tokens of the needs of those who suffer still. The afflicted offer up their sorrow, acknowledge and renounce their sins, expose their weakness to the light of God's judgment and grace." He returned the crutch to its place. "At this shrine that marks where Daniel was saved, others seek salvation."

By now the Pilgrims had closed in on us, forming a human wall about fifteen feet back. Almost all their eyes had lifted to Daniel, still perched on Bundower's shoulders. "How come they're crying?" Daniel asked.

"They weep with joy," Volpe said. "They've been waiting for you, some for so long."

"Waiting for what?" the Chief asked.

As if in response, a small woman stepped away from the crowd, out into the open space between them and us. She wasn't old, but she took tiny steps as if she were afraid she might fall, and she walked with her eyes cast to the earth. When she stood before Bundower, she timidly extended a hand clutching a photograph. It shivered with her trembling.

My brother wriggled and the Chief bent to a knee. Daniel slid off his back, came around to the trembling woman, and lifted the photo from her. Holding it with both hands, he brought it up to his face. "She looks just like you," Daniel said.

Still staring at the ground, the woman said, "Dolores is my baby sister."

"Where is she?" Daniel asked, looking around. "Didn't she want to see the festival?"

"Dolores can't leave the hospital. She would have loved to have been here herself."

"She must be real sick."

The trembling woman nodded. "Well, she smoked too many cigarettes. Now she can't breathe right by herself."

Daniel moved to give the photograph back and said, "Maybe the doctors can make her all better."

But the trembling woman held up a hand and shook her head. "I brought that here for you. Keep it. And pray for Dolores. Please." Then she turned and shuffled away, disappearing into the Pilgrim crowd and leaving Daniel with nothing to do but slide the picture into his back pocket.

"Thank you," Leo said. He settled his deformed hand on Daniel's shoulder. "This is all we ask."

Those of us circled behind Daniel — me and Bundower, my mother and Volpe and Mayor Wheeler — we all traded glances, hoping that somebody else knew for sure how to interpret what was happening. By the time I turned back to the Pilgrim congregation, a few were stepping forward from the crowd, and those behind them seemed to be falling in line. It was as if they'd choreographed this smooth movement, like they were suddenly flowing with one mind.

The second Pilgrim to come before Daniel was a man wearing a blue suit and a loosened tie. His clothes looked expensive, but that didn't keep him from dropping onto one knee in the dirt before my brother. He raked a hand through his thinning hair before he spoke. "When I was young, I cheated on my wife. A dumb thing on a weekend trip. I never told her I was unfaithful."

I'm not sure Daniel knew what "unfaithful" meant, but he understood "cheated" and knew that the man had done something wrong. He shrugged his small shoulders and said, "When you hurt somebody, you should say you're sorry."

The man jerked his head side to side. "But I can't. She passed away. Last November. Before that, I was close to telling her. I swear it. But then she started getting weak. Once she was diagnosed, once we knew she wouldn't make it to the new year, how could I tell her? All the while she was wasting away in that bed, she kept patting my hand, telling me what a good man I was, telling me how I was her love forever."

Everyone in the fairy fort was silent. Even those watching along the rim above, the ones who'd followed us from the field, were still, and I wondered if they could hear what was being said at the rock. Daniel said, "Maybe she can she forgive you from heaven."

The man looked up, tears rimming his red eyes.

Daniel said, "Your wife can still hear you. Maybe she's even listening right now. You can still say you're sorry."

The man didn't smile, but he took a deep breath and staggered to his feet. Leo took his elbow and steadied him. "Lay down your guilt, brother. Bury it here in this place." Together, they moved to the side and knelt before an upside-down tricycle with no front wheel.

The third Pilgrim was a teenage girl just younger than me. She had jet-black hair and two lip rings, so for sure she wasn't from Paradise. She giggled nervously and rocked back and forth in front of Daniel, knowing that everyone was staring at her. With a sudden movement, she rolled back one sleeve and offered a wrist thick with scars. Some of the scabs were fresh and raw. Daniel reached out and held her wrist tenderly, looking at the wounds. The girl forced a laugh and said, "I do it to myself. When my parents are asleep. In my bathroom so there's no mess."

"Don't that hurt?" Daniel asked.

She nodded. "That's why I do it. But I want to stop. I really, really want to stop."

Daniel hugged her around her waist, pressing his face into her belly. "Please quit doing that." When he stepped back, she wiped a finger under one eye, smearing black mascara across her cheek. Then she wandered off, drawing a steak knife from her back pocket and dropping it into the pile of sacred artifacts.

"Thank you, merciful Christ!" Volpe shouted, and her cry was echoed by others, both in the fairy fort and, strangely, along the rim above. Still next to the man in the suit, Leo grinned at me.

The procession of afflicted circled around the fist-shaped rock. A thin lady with sunken cheeks and veins rising from her neck told Daniel she made herself throw up after she ate because she thought she looked fat. A father tightly gripped the hand of his toddler son, a sweetly smiling boy who couldn't hear or speak. An olive-skinned woman pressed her hands together in prayer and said with a thick accent, "Uncle stomach very sick." A lady wearing glasses on a chain offered Daniel her crooked fingers, plagued for years by arthritis. Clutching a worn Bible to his chest, a trucker said he'd run over a man in a gas station in Virginia fifteen years ago. Rather than stopping to get help, he sped off in a panic. When he finished his confession, he joined the adulterous man, who was still on his knees.

Not everybody in the line was a total stranger. At one point Jeff's father stepped up and, without saying a word, emptied the liquor from his monogrammed silver flask. He tossed it onto the pile and it clattered up against a Ouija board. Jim and Sally Guth appeared as well. Lifting Daniel's hand to her belly, she asked, "Can you feel that life?"

Jim raised his eyebrows. "Right now, our baby is half the size of a sweet pea. That's what the doc said. Thank you."

After waiting patiently, each Pilgrim came forward. I'd guess about half made a request for relief from physical suffering, either for themselves or a loved one. The other half confessed some secret sin and sought penance or outright absolution. Some wanted to give Daniel a letter or a tiny gift. One lowered a necklace over Daniel's head, then centered its gold cross on his chest.

As the cured and the penitent moved away, most wept, a few laughed. Three or four fainted and had to be carried off by Leo and a couple of the Pilgrims that I recognized from the white robe choir.

All the while I kept a close eye on Daniel, looking for trembling or sweat, any sign of physical strain. But he seemed fine, better than fine, even. My brother seemed energized.

I watched all this the same way you observe a dream in your deepest sleep. None of it seemed quite real. I found myself focusing on the Pilgrims' faces, trying to read their needs. Leo had suggested that they'd all come because they believed they needed some kind of healing. But up close, I saw something else mixed in with all that brightness and hope: desperation. And it occurred to me that nobody believes in miracle cures until they've exhausted their other options.

The strangest thing is that for just a second I swore I saw myself out there among the Pilgrims wrapping around the fist-shaped rock, waiting in line for an audience with Daniel. Maybe it was just somebody who looked a whole lot like me. Maybe it was a hallucination brought on by my jealousy, the wish I resented even as I felt it, that I too could feel the Pilgrims' faith. Whatever the source of that vision, it got me wondering what I would say, what healing I would request from my brother if I were a true believer.

"Where are they all coming from?" Bundower asked, snapping me from that fantasy.

From our side, Leo answered the Chief by pointing up to the ridge, where, here and there, a festivalgoer was descending the slope into the fairy fort. People who'd driven to Paradise expecting nothing more than cotton candy and carnival games were coming forward to have the stains lifted from their souls. It was when I was looking at these folks, the ones watching from above, that I saw an out-of-towner holding a video camera in one hand, and even from a hundred feet away I could see the green light blinking. We were being filmed. It wasn't hard to imagine the footage making its way onto the six o'clock news up at WPBE, and from there I wondered if the networks or the satellite news stations would pick up the story. I pictured Paradise overrun with pilgrims, and Daniel at the center.

I was trying to think of a way to get my hands on the camera when the Abernathys stepped out from around the fist-shaped rock. Mr. Abernathy was cradling Miracle, wrapped snug in a pink blanket. Mrs. Abernathy walked beside him. Volpe and my mother rushed over to embrace their friend.

"Grace," my mother said. "You should have kept that baby at home."

"No," Mrs. Abernathy said back, her eyes hazy and light, focused on Daniel. "Of all people, we had to come."

They approached Daniel and bent down so he could see Miracle. Her scrunched-up face was peaceful as she slept. He asked permission to give her a kiss. "I'll be gentle," he promised, and he leaned in.

I guess that the Abernathys had gone mostly unrecognized among the Pilgrims, because close by, those waiting in line began to whisper:

"That's the child, the baby Daniel brought back to life."

"She wasn't breathing for two hours."

"The girl is a sign sent by God."

These rumblings rolled quickly back through the congregation, which had been lulled into a kind of slumber. Now they woke, anxious and agitated.

"What's happening at the rock?"

"We can't see!"

"Wait your turn!"

Just like that, as fast as an August thunderstorm can overtake a blue sky, the orderly procession broke down and the people began to surge forward. Those already healed and those still waiting bumped up against one another, straining to get a look at the miracle baby. Bundower stepped between the Abernathys and the crowd, spread his arms wide, and said, "Let's maintain a safe perimeter. Give these good people some breathing room."

"Let us see the girl's birthmark!" someone shouted.

"Does Miracle really speak in tongues?"

We retreated into the rock, stepping our way back through the remnants of broken lives. My mother pulled Daniel inside her arms and I stood in front of him.

Leo raised his voice and said, "There's no need for this. Daniel's gift is for everyone." Some of the Pilgrims who had been in the choir with Leo helped make a little wall around us, so the crowd couldn't press in farther.

But before long everyone seemed to be shouting, and all the racket woke up Miracle. She started wailing, a sound that rose and echoed around us, as if the forest itself were suddenly in pain. The Chief looked back at me and his face seemed a little concerned. But I wasn't really worried. Until I saw Batman.

Not Batman himself, but Batman pajamas. Black and gray fabric, a patch of yellow from his chest emblem. In the Pilgrim crowd, five feet from me, stood Scarecrow, and hanging around his neck like a scarf were Daniel's bloodied Batman pajamas, the ones he wore the night of Miracle's birth. My mother must've thrown them in the garbage.

Unlike the rest of the pilgrims, he wasn't pushing or shouting. He was perfectly still. Beneath sprawling wiry eyebrows, his stare narrowed on my brother.

"Chief!" I yelled above the din. "Somebody over here you need to meet."

Bundower glanced over, followed my eyes, and saw what I saw. His hand swung quick along his hip, then stretched over his head, shoving his pistol high in the air. Even in the dull gray light, the metal gleamed. The Pilgrims froze, eyes wide in surprise and shock. The Chief didn't fire his gun, and I wondered again if it was even loaded. "Okay then," Bundower said without emotion. "Now that I have your undivided attention. You will all step away calmly."

The Pilgrims backed off without turning around, just a few feet really, enough to show the Chief they understood he meant business. But Scarecrow stood his ground, and as the crowd receded, he was left out in the open. I was the closest one to him.

The Chief brought his pistol down and, holding it with both hands, he aimed it directly at the man. "Kneel down and lace your fingers behind your head. Now."

"Wait!" Leo shouted, and Pilgrims in the crowd backed farther away. A few people screamed.

The Scarecrow didn't take his eyes off Daniel, and even when I stepped in front of my brother, the man's crooked gaze seemed to pierce my body. Not even glancing at the Chief, he said, "You cannot harm this body for it is a temple of truth. Your bullets are but smoke." He reached up and stroked the pajamas the way a baby rubs a soft blanket for comfort. "I need to lay my hands on the boy, feel his flesh to be sure his heart is true."

"You need to get on your knees," the Chief said.

But the man ignored him.

"Please," Leo said to Bundower. "It's clear he isn't well." He held up his open palms to the Scarecrow. "Gentle brother," he said. "You believe the Lord has called you to this place?"

Scarecrow scratched at his shoulder and shook his head, his eyes still fixed on Daniel. "I do not merely believe. I know. He speaks to me even now and I do His bidding without question. My soul is freed from doubt. The boy must be tested."

Over my shoulder, I heard Daniel sniffle. "Andi," he said. "Something bad's gonna happen."

Well, that was enough for me. I turned around and took his hand. Crouching behind him, her arms still locked around his body, my mother said, "Ann, what are you doing?"

"I'm taking Daniel home. He ain't safe here."

I expected her to disagree, but she relaxed her arms and I tugged my brother free. "C'mon, Little Man," I said. "We're out of here."

I had no plan, but I knew for sure that the Chief wouldn't let Scarecrow follow us, and I didn't even look back as I led Daniel out the way we came, away from the fist-shaped rock.

Since the Pilgrims had crowded in close, there wasn't really a clear path out of the fairy fort. They were crammed shoulder to shoulder, and I had to squeeze past. Some reached out to touch Daniel, maybe hoping to steal a quick blessing. He was sniffling hard, wiping his nose across his sleeve. "What about Mom?" he asked me.

"She'll be fine," I said. "She's with the Chief."

With most of the people still focused on the action around the rock, our retreat was going just fine until we reached the edge of the crowd. Up to that point, we'd only been seen by the Pilgrims we bumped past, and even with them, it didn't seem to register that I was taking Daniel away. But when we began climbing the slope out of the fairy fort, we were in plain sight of everyone — all those watching from the rim above and all the Pilgrims gathered below. Over my shoulder, I glanced again at the fist-shaped rock, where Bundower stood next to Scarecrow, who was apparently now handcuffed with his arms behind his back. One squinting eye focused on me and he yelled, "That liar girl's spiteful heart will bury his light!"

Now a new truth seemed to dawn on the Pilgrims: I was stealing their savior. A few pointed at us and some began shouldering their way through the crowd, in pursuit.

"Let's go, Daniel," I said, and we climbed, bending forward.

When we neared the top of the ridge, there were already two or three Pilgrims at the bottom of the slope starting up. I told myself that once we reached the rim, we'd be safe among normal people, the ones who'd followed us away from the festival out of simple curiosity.

But when we reached the level ground of the forest and stood up, a bearded man I didn't even recognize blocked my path and said, "These people need Daniel."

The bearded man's voice was deep with hurt and betrayal.

Even worse, all around him I noticed festivalgoers, just ordinary folks who'd come in for a little carnival, giving me looks like I was the worst person in the world. Down in the fairy fort, some of the Pilgrims were wailing.

"Don't leave us!"

"We didn't do anything wrong."

I looked at the bearded man and started to say something, but his mind was made up, and at that point, mine was too. So I just squeezed Daniel's hand again and pulled him around the bearded guy, down the path, and toward the field. Daniel was in kind of a daze and didn't say anything. I pretended not to hear the voices gathering behind us.

My father taught me that if you ever come across a bear in the forest, the thing to do is walk away. Slow and calm. Nothing activates a bear's attack sense more than seeing something running. Instinct takes over and it can't help but pursue — that's just in its blood.

What I learned that day in the forest is that a mob is much like a bear. My first mistake was looking back. Daniel and I were in the clear, a good ways down the winding path of cut stumps, just entering the orchard of wild apple trees. But there was this tingle in the back of my neck, like something was right behind us. I glanced over my shoulder, but nobody was following us. A group had huddled around the bearded man. How many were Pilgrims and how many were just festivalgoers I couldn't tell. But they weren't moving, just watching us go. Even at a distance, I could see the anger in their faces, and I realized with a start that Daniel and I were completely alone in the forest. The Chief and Leo were as good as a million miles away.

To tell you the truth, I don't even remember making the decision to run. Maybe Jeff's right and it's my nature. But all at once my legs were in motion and instead of just holding Daniel's hand, I was yanking him hard by the wrist. Taking off, bolting like that, that was my second mistake. Because just like the bear, the mob couldn't help but pursue.

Somebody let loose with a good whooping yell and when I looked back again, it was like a dam had burst. People were flowing down the hill, along the trail and through the trees, charging after me and my brother.

We had a good lead on them, plus we had fear on our side, and nothing makes you run faster. Daniel and I hopped over fallen logs and scooted around stumps and rocks and all the while I never let go of his hand. I didn't risk looking back again, afraid I might fall, but soon enough I could hear their voices as they yelled:

"In the name of Christ Jesus, stop!"

"His gift is meant for us all!"

"Bring him back to us!"

At the time, I thought that was the most scared I could be. Before the night was over, I'd learn better.

But right then I just ran, through the broken stone wall and then past the stage and into the field where Paradise Days was still going on. It seemed impossible to me that with everything happening at the fairy fort, people could still be buying funnel cake and playing horseshoes, but plenty were. Of course that all stopped as I came ripping through with a roaring gang of Pilgrims not far behind me. You might think that the Pilgrims would have been slowed down, but instead the other festivalgoers fell in and started running too, just to be sure they didn't miss anything, I guess. So basically it felt like we were at the front end of a cattle stampede. The Pilgrims were gaining on us, and even though I wasn't sure what they would do if they caught us, I thought it was best not to find out.

I didn't have the keys to Bundower's car, and there was no safe place I could duck us into to hide. I'd been running blind. Just as this all came clear to me, the hot air balloon rose up before us, and I pictured Daniel and me climbing in and escaping into the sky. The wicker basket was on the ground, with just the guy running the ride. But I also saw the ropes, thick as power cables, binding the balloon to the ground. We'd be no better than the raccoons chased up a tree by Bundower and Pinkerton.

So, too terrified to stop, I pulled Daniel past the balloon and past the statue of FDR, thinking vaguely of running along the beach and trying to lose our pursuers in the forest.

And then, just as the grass beneath us gave way to dirty sand, a high, whining roar rose from the lake and I saw Jeff Cedars racing toward land on his Jet Ski. I charged into the lake, lifting my legs as high as I could, tugging Daniel, who was by now practically dead weight. Just behind us, I heard splashing, but I didn't look back.

I was hip deep in the water and I'd just taken Daniel into my arms when Jeff ripped past us like we weren't even there. Confused, I turned my head just in time to see him crank the Jet Ski hard, spinning it 180 degrees and dousing the Pilgrims with water. They dove for cover, and Jeff scooted the idling Jet Ski up alongside us. "C'mon!" he yelled.

I hoisted Daniel up onto the seat, then climbed up quick and wrapped my arms around my brother. As soon as I grabbed the sides of Jeff's life jacket, he twisted his wrist and the rear of the Jet Ski sank as we accelerated. Behind us, the soaked Pilgrims rose and stood knee-deep in the water, lifting their arms at us, pleading. I didn't recognize any of them. The whole mob spread out along the shoreline, watching our retreat. Above them, the balloon floated to the end of its tether and hung, but we zipped across the surface of the lake like a skipped stone, completely free.

CHAPTER THIRTEEN

About six months after we got chased into Paradise Lake by the Pilgrim mob, I read an account of that day on one of the websites that had started popping up all over the Internet. Someone who claimed to have "interviewed a dozen sworn eyewitnesses" described Daniel levitating onto the fist-shaped boulder and singing a healing song in a language no one could recognize. According to this account, among those cured by Daniel were a blind woman and a child crippled since birth. Furthermore, his singing drove a demonic spirit from a possessed man who'd tried to attack him with a hatchet. In this fantasy, when my brother's work was done, white rose petals showered down from a clear blue sky and the faithful lifted Daniel on their shoulders and carried him to the lake in celebration.

I remember getting angry when I read it, just like I did whenever I'd first come across one of these things, which is why these days I don't look at them at all. But to be honest, I knew it was a better story than what actually happened. It's more exciting for one thing. And for another, it's got a clear lesson — that God gave Daniel the power to perform miracles and everybody was happy about it. That's something people want from a story, a neat little theme. You learn that much in grade school, or even before then — when you read fairy tales. Take Red Riding Hood. She learned not to talk to strangers, especially wolves. There's always got to be a moral at the end that's supposed to help you somehow, teach you a lesson or show you how to see the world more clearly. Jesus had this figured out, which is why He always told parables to get His point across.

I suppose it's fair if right now you're wondering what the theme of this story I'm telling is, and just for the record, I'm still working on that myself.

See, when I was a kid, I believed in everything. The Easter Bunny and Santa Claus and everything else little children accept without question. Be honest, you know what I'm talking about. Can you remember the simple wonder of it, settling into the warmth beneath your blankets with the certainty that somewhere in the night, while you were dreaming peacefully, a fairy woman — white dress, glowing wand — would descend from some distant heaven, pluck the dead tooth from under your pillow, and leave a bright coin in its place? It seems absurd now. But more than just these childish fantasies, I believed in my mother and my father and the wonderful village of Paradise, and I believed in Jesus. Up at the UCP, I'd read those stories from the Bible and feel their magical power and everything made perfect sense.

That day on the lake, as Jeff skimmed the water, things had never made less sense. My mind tumbled in a state of total confusion. Because back in that fairy fort, for a time it seemed to me that Daniel was indeed capable of miracles. I was happy to see that lady with arthritis open and close her hands without pain, thrilled to see the determination in Mr. Cedars' eyes as he gave up that flask. But once the Pilgrims began shouting, that faith fluttered away, and in its wake I felt like a gullible idiot, a child tricked into thinking a magician could saw a woman in half.

"Where should I go?" Jeff shouted back, twisting his head to the side.

I couldn't think of an answer, so I didn't speak, and he kept going the way he was.

For a while I just squeezed Daniel, sandwiched between us, and stared down at the water flashing past. I imagined Irene McGinley beneath the lake, still roped to her church, bound by a faith more powerful than any I could conceive. I imagined her shaking her head, ashamed of my weakness. Really, who I was to say that Daniel wasn't blessed? What if everybody else was right and I was wrong? I thought of the sick and desperate people in need of healing, back at Paradise Days, up at St. Jude's, all over, everywhere. One thing there will never be a shortage of in the world is suffering.

On the water, we zoomed past the compound and McGinley's Cove and I settled my head onto Daniel's shoulder and asked if he was okay. He didn't move and didn't speak, like he'd been struck dumb, a kind of reverse miracle.

I didn't realize where Jeff had decided to take us until he turned toward land and aimed the Jet Ski at the rickety boardwalk of Action Water Thrill Ride City. He cut the engine so we coasted in, and the nose barely bumped the piers along the forest's edge. The stillness that fell over us was peaceful and terrible. Seemed nobody wanted to move or talk, so we just sat silently, catching our breath as the water rocked beneath us.

Finally a woodpecker jackhammered at a tree somewhere in the forest. This snapped the frozen moment and Jeff said, "I figured it best if we were someplace nobody would look. Think this is all right for now?"

"Fine," I told him. "Perfect."

Jeff climbed up onto the boardwalk and tied us off. I passed Daniel to him and then he reached down for my hand and pulled me up. Kneeling in front of my brother on the sunbaked deck, I looked into his glazed and tired eyes. Maybe it was the overcast sky, but the brown of his irises seemed almost black. "Are you okay?"

He chewed on his lip and blinked a few times.

"Daniel!" I snapped, and his eyes focused on me. "Are you okay?"

He nodded his head, but still didn't say anything.

"Are you hurt?" I asked, and he closed his eyes and moved his head side to side.

Jeff had walked to the water's edge and broken free a few small branches. He returned and draped them over the Jet Ski. "Camouflage," he explained.

I scanned the skies. "You expecting helicopters?"

"I don't know what to expect. I'm the guy with no idea what's going on, remember? I was out trying to drum up some business, doing tricks on the Jet Ski, and then I saw you hauling ass at the front end of a riot. Let's get out of sight," he said. "Then you can fill me in."

In silence he led us down the boardwalk to a corner of the cyclone fence, a section of which had been peeled back a long time ago. We scooted through and crossed the giant sandbox where weeds sprang from filthy sand. At the kiddie pool, the ten-foot plastic mushrooms that used to shelter children were now coated with so much mold and scum that they seemed alive. Even though they'd drained the large central pool for safety, enough rainwater had gathered to form a murky pond. Something, a groundhog or a rabbit, had dropped in and drowned. The tightened skin of the corpse, ripe and bloated, seemed ready to burst.

I gripped Daniel's hand a little tighter when I caught him staring, and we passed the concrete Snax Stand with THIS IS PARADISE? spray painted on the side. Making our way to the back, we jumped a fence and took a shortcut through the Around the World in 18 Holes miniature golf course, which apparently had suffered its own miniature catastrophes. The Leaning Tower of Pisa rested on its side between the pyramids and a sphinx, and the Eiffel Tower had snapped in half. At Mount Rushmore, Lincoln's face had washed off, revealing the chicken-wire skeleton beneath. Washington looked nervous. One by one, we stepped over the Great Wall of China.

After hopping a final fence, we reached our destination: the Grand Carousel. Just ahead of us were the entrance gates with their one-way turnstiles. From so deep in the park, you could barely even see the lake, and it was unlikely that anyone floating by would be able to spot us. Jeff headed straight to one of the benches they have on the carousel for grandparents or people who just want a gentler ride. Despite the years of neglect, the bench was still somehow shiny blue. He turned to my brother and said, "Yo, Daniel, you want to just lie down for a few minutes?"

At first, Daniel didn't seem to hear him, but then he crawled up onto the bench and curled into a fetal tuck. Jeff handed him the life vest he'd been wearing. "Put this under your head."

Daniel took the vest and used it as a pillow.

I knelt down again, bringing myself eye to eye with him. "Little Man," I said, "tell me you're all right."

Without smiling, Daniel closed his eyes. His freckled cheeks were still flushed red.

Jeff rested a hand on my shoulder and cocked his head to the side. "C'mon. Just let him sleep."

I followed Jeff and we zigzagged around the curve of the carousel. About half the poles were empty, and after a few seconds I realized that all the traditional horses were gone, sold off, I guess. All that remained were these goofy sea creatures no other amusement park would want, a purple dolphin and a green shark side by side, a polka-dotted octopus whose bubblehead you could straddle. Jeff climbed atop a bright yellow sea horse and I settled on an orange walrus. We were about halfway around the carousel, out of Daniel's earshot even if he wasn't yet asleep.

"All right," Jeff said. "So what the hell happened?"

I raked a hand through my hair, then I took a long breath and told him the story the best I could, starting with Bundower being assigned as our escort to Paradise Days and including parts about Leo that I thought were important. Jeff's eyes opened wide when I got to the parade of afflicted. I finished up with the Scarecrow who'd stolen Daniel's pajamas and my great escape through the forest and the field and out into the water, where he came in.

"Running was a major screwup," I told him.

"You don't know that," he said. "If you'd stayed, that crowd could've closed in around you. It could've been a whole lot worse."

I glanced in Daniel's direction. "Worse?"

Jeff shook his head. "You can't blame yourself for doing what you thought was right."

We sat in silence for a bit, each clutching our gold pole as if the ride was about to begin. In my mind, I could hear the cheerful carousel music, and I even remembered a flash from opening day, Daniel and me waiting in line for this very ride. But those pleasant memories weren't enough to block the question that kept haunting me. I turned to Jeff. "What if I'm wrong about Daniel?"

"Come again?" he said.

"Do you think Daniel might be what they say? I'm asking you."

"Come on, Andi, that's not a fair question."

"Fair or not, do you think Daniel's special?"

"Special?" he repeated. "Sure."

"Okay. You think he can make miracles happen?"

Jeff tilted his forehead into the pole. "No. Maybe. I don't know."

"That's what's got me worried. It could be that Mr. Abernathy and Volpe are right and I'm the one who's nuts. What if I'm keeping Daniel from people who need him?"

Jeff seemed to be staring at his own reflection in the shiny pole. "Andi," he finally said, "I don't know what to tell you. My dad, he really does seem changed."

"He was up there," I said. "At the fairy fort."

"My dad?"

I nodded.

"He had the chills so bad yesterday I had to get a winter blanket down. That's why we called in Jess to help out at the festival. I thought my dad was at home in bed."

"Nope," I said. "He was giving praise to my brother."

"That sounds pretty screwed up."

"Yeah," I said. "But . . ." I couldn't finish the thought. And my mind turned again to all those people who'd come to see Daniel, the sick and the guilty, the nights they'd stayed awake hoping to one day feel his power and have their lives made better. I thought about what Leo said, about wounds you can see and wounds you can't, and how everybody needed healing. I looked over at Jeff and said, "Let's say Daniel could pray for you, ask God for any wish and it would be granted. You could have anything you wanted. Like with a genie or a fairy godmother. What would you wish for?"

Jeff scratched his chin and looked away from me, staring out into the ruined amusement park. Beyond the slides and fence, beneath the gray sky, the lake looked like a sheet of black glass. "I think a lot," he said, "about how things could've been. You know. With us."

There was a soft look on his face, like back in the dressing room at the school. That woodpecker rattled away again, deeper into the woods.

"Yeah," I surrendered. "Me too sometimes."

Jeff turned back in my direction but still avoided direct eye contact. "So I guess that I'd wish Daniel never fell into that hole."

This answer surprised me, and from my face he could tell I was taken off guard.

I said, "Yeah. Everything changed kind of fast."

"Well, you sure did."

"What's that mean?"

Jeff could tell I was a little hot, but now he looked right in my eyes. "You got hard, Andi. Somewhere along the way, you got plain hard."

"Maybe I just grew up."

"Whatever you say."

We both fell into an awkward silence. I began to regret getting Jeff involved at all. Like I said, after Daniel got pulled out of that well, we never really talked about what happened beforehand. We just kind of stopped hanging around each other, and then at the end of that crazy summer, he was off to Penn State.

But there's a little more to our story. Now look, I don't want you to think I lied to you earlier, but when I told you that Jeff and I were just walking in the woods and talking on the day that Daniel fell into the well, that wasn't the whole truth. Jeff and I, we were holding hands. We'd come up into the woods to be together, and we only brought Daniel because my dad made us. We'd been spending time together in one of the empty cabins, and our evenings there had become more intense. As the time for him to leave for college drew near, we both felt the energy between us building toward something inevitable. Resisting that final temptation was getting harder and harder.

That day, walking with Daniel through the fairy fort, Jeff and I kept squeezing hands and trading looks, sending secret signals. The fact is that out of the blue, while three-year-old Daniel chased a lizard through the leaves, I pulled Jeff behind one of the bigger rocks. Right away he put his arms around me and I brought my mouth to his. After we kissed, he warmed his cheek against mine and whispered, "Tonight?" and I knew what he meant. I felt light and excited and scared, and I nodded my consent.

That's when we realized we'd lost track of Daniel.

The rest, how at first we thought he was hiding and how frantically we searched and everything that happened after, I already told you. But now maybe you understand why things got so weird between me and Jeff. Because neither one of us told anybody the full truth, and nobody else ever knew it, until now.

And sure, it had occurred to me that maybe God was punishing me. The Bible teaches that sinning in thought is the same as sinning in deed. So it could be that what happened to Daniel was my punishment for lust. Maybe the whole thing was my fault. But I'd never told Jeff about the responsibility I felt, and that day on the carousel, when Jeff told me what he'd wish for, I thought that maybe I wasn't the only one who felt guilty.

A dark blue sailboat cut slowly across the lake, way out in the middle of the water.

Once again, it was Jeff who broke the silence. "So since you're all grown up and everything," he said, "what would you change? If you could wish for anything?"

I looked back over at Daniel, tucked up tight on that bench. I thought about wishing my father back, but if he didn't want to be here, I didn't want him here. I thought about making Scarecrow vanish, but with all the rabid eyes I saw in that mob, I knew there'd always be other people to take his place. I thought about once again possessing that perfect belief I'd had when I was a kid, the absolute faith that my parents loved me and God was in Heaven looking out for me and that everything would be okay. But even after what I'd witnessed in the fairy fort, I couldn't bring myself to accept this. It felt like going backward. So I came back to the thing I wanted most. "I'd wish everyone would just leave Daniel alone."

Jeff knew what I meant. He said, "So you still think the Plan will work?"

"It has to," I told him. "There's just no other way."

He rocked back and forth on his sea horse, processing what I'd said. "Then we're still on for tomorrow?" he finally asked.

I shook my head. "No. We can't wait. We've got to do it tonight."

Later, when Daniel woke up, I was watching over him. His eyes opened to me staring into his face, but he didn't seem surprised. It was like he was expecting to see me there. "Hey, Andi," he said, and I was so glad to hear his voice again that I almost hugged him. But I didn't want to make a big deal about it, so I just answered, "Hey, Little Man."

He rubbed at his eyes, sat up, and looked around. "Where's Jeff?"

"He'll be back. Did you have a good nap?"

"Uh-huh," he said. He yawned. "I'm hungry."

"Me too," I told him. "We'll eat soon. We have to wait here."

"Okay," Daniel said without argument or complaint. "Andi, I got to pee."

I pointed toward the chained entrance gate, the parking lot, and the forest beyond it. "Nobody's around. It'll be fine."

I faced the park to give him privacy, and when he shuffled back over after he was done, he zipped his fly up and said, "How come those people were chasing us?"

I thought about it. "Well, they were confused."

"They think I can pray miracles."

"That's about the size of it. But listen. Me and you and Jeff, we're going to play a trick on those people. On everybody."

Daniel looked at me, eager as always to listen. I'm not sure he understood everything I told him about the Anti-Miracle Plan, but he said he liked to pretend and he'd do what I wanted. To Daniel, it was all a game. Sweet, sweet boy.

By the time Jeff returned, Daniel and I were standing in front of the Taj Mahal, using a stick to putt a pinecone through the hollowed-out onion dome. We all circled around a picnic table. From a Penn State backpack, Jeff pulled some sandwiches, a couple cans of Coke. When Daniel said thanks, Jeff did a double take and said, "Cat gave your tongue back, huh?"

Daniel shrugged and bit into his ham sandwich.

I cracked a Coke and reached for the sandwich Jeff handed me. "All we got to do now is wait for dark."

CHAPTER FOURTEEN

An hour after the sun's glow finally faded from the sky, Jeff ferried Daniel and me up the lake, idling the Jet Ski low and quiet. He stuck to the western bank, where we'd appear to anyone as little more than shifting shadows beneath the full moon. Because we were moving so slowly, I didn't need to wrap my arms around my brother to hold on. But I did. For a while I even stretched forward enough to slide my hands along Jeff's ribs. Then, beneath the rumble of the engine, I thought I heard someone calling my name from far off. At first I guessed it was Irene McGinley or my imagination, but then Daniel said, "Hey, Andi, how come Mom's yelling?"

Jeff killed the motor and the Jet Ski coasted to a stop, and together we listened to the silence. From far off, the noises of Paradise Days sounded tiny, like a festival of toys. Then a distant voice boomed, "Ann! Daniel!" My mother's call rose from the blackness of the woods on the east side of the lake. As we turned in that direction, lights flickered a hundred feet deep in the forest. Bundower's police cruiser slow-rolled around a curve in Roosevelt Road. My mother's voice was broadcasting from the speaker on top of the prowling car. The spotlight attached to the Chief's door shone like a tiny lighthouse beacon, casting trees into silhouette as it sliced through the forest, sweeping a white disk along the shoreline and out into the water. Jeff reached for the key, but I whispered, "No. They'll hear the ignition."

He nodded, then a moment later tilted his head. Quietly he and I swung our legs over the seat and slipped into the lake, where the cool water felt crisp and good. "Get down flat," Jeff told Daniel, who did as he was told.

The searchlight swooped around us, but it never came all that near, and we hung together in the rocking water until the Chief passed. Down the lake, we heard my mother's voice echoing over the water, growing weaker with each broadcast. Jeff and I waited a bit longer to be sure, then we climbed back aboard.

"Why does Mom sound so sad?" Daniel asked.

"She's okay," I said.

Jeff added, "She doesn't know we're playing hide-and-seek."

"Just go, all right?" I told him. "The sooner we get on with this, the sooner we'll be done."

Jeff faced forward and the seat beneath me shivered with the engine's return. We started slowly ahead, but now I kept my arms around Daniel.

I pictured my mother next to Bundower in his cruiser. Like Daniel, I could tell from the cracks in her voice that she'd been crying, and I wondered if Bundower had tried to comfort her, placed a warm palm over her clenched fist. I wished there were some way I could let her know that I'd come up with a way to fix everything.

Across the black water, we passed by the waiting mouth of McGinley's Cove and then, a quarter mile south of our compound, Jeff cut across the lake and brought us in close to the eastern shoreline. I stepped off into the murky crud along the bank. "Look," I said, "I didn't mean to snap."

"No sweat. This whole thing is totally crazy."

"Okay," I said, "I should be at your folks' place in like twenty minutes, tops."

Daniel said, "I want to come with you."

"Stay with Jeff," I said. "I'll see you soon." Earlier, I'd told Jeff to take Daniel to Gayle's for the night if things did go wrong, and I tried to remind him with a hard look.

I could see enough of his eyes to know he got my message, and he nodded. "All right then. You just get there. And be careful."

"No other way to be," I answered. Then I turned to the black woods and he swung the Jet Ski back the way we came.

In my soggy sneakers and soaked clothes, I bushwhacked through the forest, avoiding the trail. The darkness made my progress slow. I held my hands in front of me as if I were blind, keeping limbs from scratching my face too badly, but my feet kept snagging on roots and bramble, rocks and fallen branches. I tripped more than once, went down pretty hard in a prickle bush, came up with my palms bloodied a bit. If I were given to superstition, I'd have thought the forest was trying to hold me back. Still, I stayed clear of the well-worn paths since I didn't want to wander into anyone else out looking for us. A few times I again thought I heard someone calling my name, but when I'd pause and try to focus, the voices would disappear.

After fifteen minutes of shuffling and stumbling, I finally reached the edge of the compound and crouched behind a pine tree down by the salt lick. Up at the main house, lights glowed from the kitchen and the front porch, but I was pretty sure I was alone. Still, I crept along the woods and got what I needed from the shed. I knew where everything was by touch and piled it into a backpack. At my cabin, I changed into a dry T-shirt and shorts and traded my soggy sneakers for dry ones.

When I snuck up the hill, I found the red scooter Volpe motors around town on. Since my mother was out patrolling with Bundower, Volpe must have been recruited to keep the home fires burning, in case we simply returned. I scanned the house but saw no sign of her. She had to be around somewhere, close enough to hear the Skylark's engine for sure. I couldn't stop her from knowing I'd been there, but I could keep her from telling anybody else. Without feeling too guilty, I eased the kickstand up on the scooter and guided the bike down to the shed. In case my mother had left her the keys to the truck, I deflated its two rear tires. Crouched by the rear bumper, I saw Volpe's thin figure pass before a window in the kitchen. She was talking on the phone. Quiet as I could, I made my way to the side of the house, got ahold of the phone cord, and used my father's pocketknife to slice it neatly. I sprinted up to the Skylark, climbed in, and turned the key. I heard the creaky screen door slam shut but didn't waste time looking. Only after I was heading up the driveway did I spare a glance into the rearview mirror. Sure enough, there stood Volpe in the light of the front porch, skinny arms locked on her skinny hips. My best guess was that it would take her fifteen minutes to get to the nearest house to use their phone.

Being in the car, successfully completing the first part of the Plan, made it all seem real in a way it hadn't so far. You know, you think about a thing for a long time, but then it starts to happen, and it's different somehow. The actual doing. But rattling south on Roosevelt Road, I didn't wonder if my actions were right or wrong. I'd decided it was the only way to save Daniel, and so it was what I had to do.

Just a few minutes after I left the compound, I pulled up in front of Jeff's home. He and Daniel came scuttling up from the dock. My brother crawled up onto the big front seat next to me. Jeff got in and I was backing out before he closed the door. It swung shut and he had to snap his hand back, so he shot me a look.

"I ran into some company," I said. "We've got to move."

"Yeah," he said. "I figured. On the dock we could hear your mom's voice and see the light from the Chief's patrol car. It passed below the dam and was moving its way up the far lakeshore. They had just about made it to the country club when all of a sudden it stopped."

Volpe's cell phone. I'd forgotten about it. With the bridge out, though, Bundower would need to circle almost the entire lake. He wouldn't know where to look for me, but if he drove straight through on Roosevelt Road, he could be at the cove in less than fifteen minutes.

"What's it mean?" Jeff asked.

I accelerated and said, "It means we need to haul ass. Tell me again what you're going to say later."

Jeff recited the lines we'd rehearsed back at the carousel. "Anderson said she was going to Canada, or Mexico, someplace far away that never heard of Daniel. I tried to talk her out of it but she said it was the only way."

"That's good," I told him. "Lay it on thick."

"I want to go to Mexico," Daniel said.

I ignored him. "Make me sound crazy, all right? And later on, if nobody catches on right away, don't crack too soon. Give it a couple days at least until you come clean and rat me out."

We sped the last mile in silence, and as soon as I pulled the Skylark over at the Lookout, we climbed out. I grabbed the hacksaw from the trunk and handed it to Jeff. Together we turned to the metal guardrail near the edge of the cliff. I told him, "Work on the middle post till we get down. I'll signal you with the flashlight."

"But you said we should cut through all three."

I shook my head. "There's no time."

"You get far out on those rocks," Jeff said.

I saw the care in his eyes. "Be sure the steering wheel's straight. Give it an extra shove."

We knew we had a lot to say to each other, but the clock was ticking. Daniel said, "Is it time to play our trick on everybody?"

I nodded and handed him the flashlight. "You be in charge of the lightsaber, okay, young Jedi?"

He gripped it tight with both hands and sent the tiny ball of light playing across the shifting grass. I led my brother to the side of the Lookout, where we started down the steepest trail in Paradise. "Small steps," I told him.

Behind us and above, Jeff said, "Yo, Grant. Good luck."

I looked back and couldn't see him in the night. So into the pitch darkness I said, "Yo, Cedars. Same to you."

As Daniel and I descended, I heard the grating hush of the hacksaw working against the metal. I stayed in front of Daniel on the slope so that if he did slip, I'd block him from tumbling too far down. I eased my feet one step at a time, grabbing hold of a branch here or there for balance. Now and then we had to slide on our butts for a few feet. But really, it wasn't nearly as treacherous as it had been in my memory. Every minute of the descent, I waited for the high whine of Bundower's siren.

When we reached level ground, I was surprised that I could feel the sharp bite of the rocks even through my sneakers. We passed the cave, and Daniel shone his flashlight in, but the blackness swallowed the beam. Then he turned it onto the rocks ahead of us and found a crushed washing machine on its side. We both looked up the straight cliff face.

"Who did that?" Daniel asked, and his words echoed off the walls that surrounded us. I'd forgotten about shouting out curse words here when I was a kid. Since the cove's shaped like a horseshoe, any loud sound gets bounced out onto the lake.

I took Daniel's hand and whispered, "I don't know. We have to hurry now."

I led us a safe distance out onto the stony beach, a good hundred feet or so from the base of the Lookout, practically to the lake's edge. I unzipped my backpack and pulled out the plastic tube of fake blood. While Daniel watched, I poured some into one hand and went to work, sliming the stinky red gush all over my neck and my bare arms as if I was applying suntan lotion.

"How do I look?" I asked my brother.

Daniel gave me a once-over. "Like it's Halloween."

"That'll work. Your turn."

I tipped the bottle to my hand again, making a puddle in my palm. I knelt down on the rocks and rubbed the blood into my brother's scalp. "Let's start off with a massive head wound," I told him.

The mixture oozed as I massaged it into his hair. Then I smeared his face with the phony blood, telling him to keep his eyes closed tight so none spilled in. It reminded me of when I used to give him his baths and I'd cover his eyes with a wet face cloth to keep out the shampoo.

"All right," I announced, "you look bad enough."

He reached up and touched his bloodied hair, then sniffed his stained finger. "Smells funny."

"Don't worry about the smell," I told him. I lifted the flashlight from him and said, "C'mon now. Slide around."

Still on my knees, I pulled him behind me, so I'd be between him and the crash. He crouched low and set his hands on my shoulders.

I aimed the flashlight toward the top of the Lookout and thumbed the switch two or three times. In the darkness, I couldn't see Jeff, and since he had no flashlight, there was no way I could be sure he got the signal. I thought I heard the Skylark's ignition, but I wasn't sure.

Up on the Lookout, nothing was happening, and I tried to imagine what was going on. How long could it take to drive back up the hill, put her in neutral, and get out of the way? I listened closely for the engine, and it's funny, but I never heard it, maybe because of the shape of the cove or something. Whatever the reason, I was getting worried that Jeff had been caught and was starting to stand up when the soft shine of the crooked headlights beamed over the edge of the cliff. The Skylark rumbled out into the air, and I spun around and crouched, covering Daniel with my body.

But there was no crash.

My tense muscles relaxed and I let go of Daniel, then looked over my shoulder. Two hundred feet up, the Skylark's front end leaned out into the abyss, but its belly rested on solid ground. It wasn't going to fall.

"Shit," I said, regretting it right away because Daniel was there.

I stood up and stared at the sight. In any other situation, it would have been comical. The front wheels turned slowly, as if groping for a road, and the whole car seemed to tip slightly forward. Jeff's silhouette appeared at the side of the car. He was waving his arms, though I had no idea what that meant. "Stay here," I ordered Daniel, and I hustled across the rocks.

By the time I got closer to the base of the cliff, Jeff was gone. I cupped my hands around my mouth and whisper-shouted "Yo!" High above, the Skylark seemed to hear me. Like eyes glancing downward, the headlights peered slightly in my direction and the square grille grinned my way. For a moment I was sure this was just my imagination, but then I figured out where Jeff was. He'd gone to the back of the car and was rocking it gently, gaining momentum with each teeter-totter. The nose of the Skylark dipped once, rose, then dipped deeper.

My legs didn't wait for my brain. I was charging back toward Daniel when the car came over the cliff, so I can't report if it did a nosedive or a full flip. All I know is that I was sprinting toward my brother, screaming for him to stay down, when something smacked me in the back of my leg, driving me onto the rocks.

The next thing I knew, Daniel was rubbing my hair, kneeling over me. Above him, all the constellations spread across the sky. I'd never seen so many stars. But then I smelled the smoke and I came back to where I was. Daniel said, "Your car crashed really good."

Remarkably, the Skylark was performing a kind of headstand on its own crumbled hood. Orange and white flames licked along the passenger side. Out by the lake, a hundred feet away, a tire stood on its end, perfectly still.

When I sat up, pain shot through my right leg. At first I thought I'd pulled a muscle, but when I reached down, I found a metal shard lodged in my calf like shrapnel. The blood flowed down and soaked my sock. I tugged my belt off and wrapped a tourniquet around my thigh.

Daniel asked if I was okay, and I told him everything would be fine. I almost believed it. Together we watched the fire engulf the Skylark, and the crackling flames rolled and whipped. A reddish glow spread up the walls of the cove.

A great sense of relief settled over me. The most dangerous part of the Anti-Miracle Plan was done. The burning wreckage would be seen across the lake. The explosion itself had no doubt been heard for miles. When people arrived at the Lookout, they'd survey the scene and come to the conclusion I wanted them to: In my reckless dash to escape, I'd killed us both. No one could survive a two-hundred-foot plummet.

Then we'd step out into the strobing light of emergency vehicles, bloody but whole. Word of our miraculous survival would spread like a well-fed fire. Within hours, the Pilgrims' faith would rise to a fever pitch. Volpe would call the folks at WPBE. Reporters and Pilgrims would surround St. Jude's, scanning the curtained windows for a glimpse of Daniel. They'd pelt Dr. Ghadari with questions. *When you washed the blood away, did Daniel really have no wounds?*

The only variable in the plan was how long it would take to uncover my hoax. I thought maybe the Chief or Dr. Ghadari would suspect something pretty quick, but they wouldn't go public right away. If after a day or two no one had stepped forward, Jeff was primed to point the finger. Plagued by a guilty conscience, he'd confess that he and I had tried to trick everyone. At first, I'd deny it all, but under pressure I'd finally give in too, surrender the hacksawed guardrail and the tube of prop blood as incontrovertible self-incrimination. All the Pilgrims and true believers would look like fools. People would suspect every grand act ever attributed to Daniel, all the way back to when this started. Nobody in Paradise or anywhere else would dare risk the embarrassment of believing in him again, and the Pilgrims would leave our town with their heads low, never to return. My brother's days as a miracle worker would be forever ended. This was my absolute goal.

Sitting with one knee bent and my bleeding leg stretched out, with Daniel standing next to me, I pictured the day in the future when no one sought his blessing. A strange, abiding peace welled up inside my chest. The fire and the smoke, the water behind us and the stars above, everything seemed serene. Daniel asked if my leg hurt bad, but honestly, I was so glad things were nearly done that I felt no pain at all.

I was content. For those few moments.

In my memory, it's the smell that comes first. Dank and musty. Ancient and untamed. But with all the smoke in the air, the burning gas and the smoldering tire rubber, I doubt that's really possible. My brain must have borrowed the odor from later and rearranged it. So I can't say for sure what the initial sign really was. I don't remember if I first saw a hulking shape drag itself from the shadowed cave behind the fire, or if I heard rocks rattled by the great paws. All that matters is that, in an instant, everything changed.

Daniel and I weren't alone in the cove.

CHAPTER FIFTEEN

Samson didn't come right at us. Patiently, methodically, he lumbered in the general direction of the Skylark's burning corpse, entering the fire's flicker with his massive head lifted high, nose up. With each step he snorted at the air, searching for the scents that would provide some clue as to what had disturbed his slumber. Seated on the rocks, I looked up at Daniel standing beside me. His face was smothered in the false blood, and right away I wondered what it would smell like to a blind and hungry bear.

"Daniel," I whispered quick, "we got to get into the lake."

He made no sign that he'd heard me. His body froze statue-still and his eyes stayed locked on Samson. I grabbed his hand and yanked it, which brought his blank gaze down to me.

"That's Samson," Daniel said. "He ain't pretend."

I nodded and tried to sound calm. "Yeah. Now you need to get out into the lake. Quiet as you can, deep as you can. Swim out around the edge of the cove and wait for me in the forest."

Daniel shook his head. "He'll chase me."

By now the bear had crossed along the cliff face, putting the burning car between us. "Samson can't see," I whispered. "And if you're in the water, he won't be able to smell you. You'll be safe. But you got to go right now."

"You gotta come with me."

I glanced at the wreck of the Skylark and couldn't see Samson directly, but the fire cast his monstrous shadow against the cliff face. "I'll come right behind you," I told my brother. "But you've got to go first."

Daniel, who never had anything but total faith in me, said, "Come fast," and his hand slipped from mine as he started toward the lake. Willing him forward, I watched his dark form wade out into the shallows. He carefully picked his way across the sharp rocks and soon the water covered his knees, his waist. Daniel was a good swimmer, and I knew he'd make it around the cove with no trouble.

With my brother out of harm's way, I turned to my own situation. Samson stood off to the side of the Skylark now, sniffing at another tire, this one smoldering. Hoping this was enough to keep him distracted, I struggled up onto my good leg and tried to put weight on the bleeding one. Pain spiked through me and made it clear I'd either be limping or crawling to the lake.

Then a thought sparked in my head. Suppose I made it to the water? My bloody trail would only lead Samson in Daniel's direction. I looked out to the lake, where I could see my brother in water only a few feet deep, not even twenty, thirty feet out. Samson could cover that distance in seconds. Daniel needed more time.

I considered trying to lure Samson away by limping for the trail, but I couldn't guarantee he'd follow. Till Daniel was safe, I couldn't leave him unprotected. So I bit my lip at the pain in my leg and lowered myself back onto the ground, posting my body between the bear and my brother. From the rocks scattered around me, I gathered fist-sized stones and stacked them into a small pyramid at my side. Samson lost interest in the smoking rubber and began cautiously circling the fire in widening arcs. The bottom half of my right leg was warm and sticky with blood, a scent I knew would summon him by deepest instinct.

When he came across my trail, he dead-stopped. With the burning wreck behind him, he turned toward me and stared. Even though I knew he couldn't see, I didn't move. He took one step in my direction, paused, then took another. Slowly but deliberately, he began plodding my way, sweeping his great head side to side. It seemed almost like he was walking out of the flames, like the beast had been born in that open fire.

A breeze swirled in off the water and circled the cove, stirring up the flames and somehow bringing me Samson's smell. It was an awful, feral odor, not just of a wild animal but of something sickly, close to death. It made me think of rotting corpses, squirrels and birds and rabbits that I'd stumbled across in the woods. When I inhaled Samson's scent, I wondered how long it had been since this carnivore had tasted fresh kill.

My heart thumped like it was trying to break through my rib cage, and every muscle in my legs twitched with the urge to run. All I'd be able to manage was a hobble, though. So I tried to breathe easy and keep my mind steady, like in a race. I knew that heading straight for the lake would only lead Samson closer to Daniel. I'd never make it past him to the steep trail, and even if I did, he'd catch me on the hill. My only hope was to disorient him, turn his attention back to the crash maybe, then slip away into the water without him in pursuit.

I stayed quiet and still until he was about ten feet away, close enough that I could hear the scrape and click of his claws against the rocks. Slowly, I lifted a stone in each hand. I heaved one over him to the left, one to the right, and when they clattered against the other rocks, he snapped his head in each direction. For a moment, I thought he might investigate. But then, his face returned to aim straight at me. He was locked onto the scent of my blood, too close and too hungry to be fooled.

He started toward me, with his rotting breath misting the air, and his sightless pink eyes fixed on me. Hard as I could, I fastballed a rock and it thudded against his neck. His lips snarled back, and a low growl filled McGinley's Cove. I rolled to my belly and jerked myself across the rocks, reaching and pulling with my arms, flopping like a fish, thinking of nothing now but escape. The still lake spread out before me, perfectly peaceful and unconcerned.

Then a crushing weight anchored my leg, flaring white pain through my eyes. I heard a scream, realized it was mine, cocked my head back, and found Samson driving a paw onto my right knee. Blind, he stared down at the gashed calf as if he could see the ripe flesh in the moonlight. Samson swept his other paw, a blurring slash, and he shredded the muscle. A strip of something wet arced into the darkness. I twisted as much as I could and kicked my free foot into his snout. It stunned him, but he was more annoyed than hurt. In response, he pressed hard on my trapped knee, driving bone into rock. Then he opened that great jaw, a cavern of teeth, and snapped down on my leg.

Since this happened, I've read about how pain works, how your brain drowns your body with chemicals to help you endure the unendurable. It produces a natural high. So when a gazelle has its limp neck draped in the mouth of a lion and is being dragged to its death, it's actually experiencing a kind of ecstasy. Call it God's last gift to the doomed. So maybe something like this is what was happening to me on the rocks that night. I mean, I have a clear memory of Samson biting into my leg. But after that first burst of white pain, there was no agony. Instead, I was peaceful in a weird way. It was like the twilight of sleep, when you're about to slip away and you can feel the weariness of the day fading, and you know there's no sense fighting it anymore.

Maybe it's because of this sleepy sense that when I saw Daniel, I thought for sure he was a dream. His arms hung straight at his sides as he slowly rose from the shallows. Thin ripples spread out away from him. The lake had washed the false blood from him, so he was clean and pure.

Now for the record, I'm not one hundred percent, absolutely certain of anything once Samson starting working on my leg. It honestly could be that my doped-up brain imagined the sound of my brother's voice and the song that seemed to gather from the walls of the cove. I've never been able to recall any lyrics from what I heard, just the rhythm, which I can only describe as something like a lullaby. Whether Daniel really sang or not, what I know for sure is that he swam back to the rocky beach after he was safe, and because of that, Samson stopped what he was doing.

The great bear turned to my brother, and I tried to shout and grab another rock, but I don't think I made any sound at all. Dark clouds floated across my vision, and I had to concentrate just to stay awake. All I have from this part of the story are snapshot images: Daniel reaching an open hand to Samson. The bear lowering his huge head as he approached my brother. Daniel setting a gentle hand on the bear's neck. His fingers caressing the fur. Sweet Daniel smiling back at me. Then the two of them turning in unison and walking side by side together, heading toward the water, as if Daniel might lead the bear to the fairy tale land of harmony and peace.

But then a thunderclap from a cloudless sky — a rifle shot from the Lookout. The startled bear towered up on its hind legs with a roar that rattled my bones. Daniel stood his ground, holding up his hands the way a lion tamer might. At the second rifle shot, Samson flinched in pain, swung wildly, and a massive paw caught Daniel in the chest. My brother's body lifted up into the air like a tossed doll. He sailed over me and crashed to the rocks not fifteen feet away. At the water's edge, Samson collapsed in a heap. The third shot made his mighty body twitch. The fourth hit home but had no effect, as the great bear was finally dead.

"Daniel!" I screamed, already scrambling over the rocks, crawling forearm over forearm, dragging my mauled leg behind me. His body lay on its side, facing away from me, toward the fire and the cave. High above, someone was shouting from the Lookout, and I was aware of flashing lights and maybe a siren's cry. But I stayed focused on Daniel's silhouette. The tips of my fingers began to tingle, then my hands, but even after my arms went numb with cold, I drove them onto the rocks and pulled myself forward. I don't know if it was from shock or loss of blood, but each breath took more effort to draw in, until by the time I reached Daniel I wasn't breathing so much as sucking at the air. I stretched a trembling hand to his shoulder and eased him onto his back.

My brother's eyes were closed, as if he were merely asleep. But a twist in his neck made me gasp, and from an open gash on his forehead, shiny blood seeped along the side of his face. By one elbow, a jagged bone broke through the skin. "Daniel," I said. "Danny."

I hoisted myself up and leaned onto him, draped an arm over

his wet chest as if hugging him. I choked back sobs and my tears fell onto his still face. I understood that others were coming, that Bundower had surely summoned rescue workers who were on their way. But the help seemed so distant at that moment, like they'd never be able to reach us, like Daniel and I were buried together in the deepest part of the earth. I couldn't hear anything by that point, no sound at all, and my body was beginning to shiver. A darkness was gathering around us.

I settled my face onto Daniel's thin chest like a pillow, maybe to pass out, maybe to die for all I knew. His shirt smelled like the lake, dank and rich. And his chest rose and fell once, I remember that, but when I pressed my ear down, I could find no beating heart.

My eyes closed, and I tried to push the truth from my mind — that these two wrecked bodies, these two fragile lives, were entirely my fault. I couldn't stand the thought that, driven by anger and fear, I'd led my brother and me here to the edge of death.

And now it was too late.

I remember thinking those exact words and wishing for oblivion, just wanting to be gone from where I was and who I'd become. But as I sucked in what I thought might well be my last breaths, a smell came to me through the must of the lake and Samson's foul odor. Vanilla. A sweetness that had nothing to do with this place. And with my eyes still closed, I felt my hand working along Daniel's body, finding his fingers — still warm and soft. My own fingers laced together with his, squeezing so he could feel the fading life I had left, take that strength from my body if it would help him. But I knew that the power to bring him back was not within me.

I wondered, though, if it might be somewhere else. The instant this notion came to me, a low warmth began to glow in the center of my body, a bright shining that hummed with white heat. I don't remember if I spoke the words, or if I just imagined them in my mind: *If you're real then you're here right now and you can hear me and keep this sweet boy from dying. Don't punish him for my screwup. You need somebody to die tonight, you take me.* The warm feeling swelled up in my chest, filled it, and spilled outward, and my arms weren't cold anymore, and I began to feel light, weightless. *Please. Please God. He's so much better than me. Please God. There's just nothing right about Daniel dying. Let him stay.* And now it seemed I'd become the warmth itself, that there wasn't an Anderson Grant anymore at all but just the warmth extending out into forever. I still felt Daniel's chest beneath my face somehow but that was the last thing, I knew I was about to leave this behind and dissipate, surrender to a greater warmth swirling calmly all around me like an ocean, and still I kept thinking it: *Please God. Please God.*

"Annie!" my mother screamed, and I opened my eyes. Flashlight beams bobbed across the rocks as Bundower ran to Samson's corpse and my mother charged for her children, dropping down next to us, and I felt the warmth still. I had not left it behind yet. My mother wept and far off I heard the patter-thump of helicopter blades. But I turned away from all these distractions and closed my eyes a final time. I pressed my face tight to my brother's quiet chest. *Please God. Please God. Please God.* Over and over the words drummed in my mind: *Please God. Please God. Please God.*

And just before they pulled me off him, I felt it on my cheek. It resonated like the first note of a hymn breaking the silence in a cathedral, like the very start of something grand and sacred: a single pulsing beat that could only mean life.

CHAPTER SIXTEEN

The emergency helicopter flew me all the way to a trauma center in Philadelphia, where a team of surgeons battled tissue damage and massive infection for hours. Of course, I have no memory of this. Even following the operation, for a time all I have are snippets of life: a loudspeaker paging someone; a nurse yanking back a curtain; a clear tube stuck in my forearm; a doctor in a white coat standing with his back to me. These mixed with nightmare fragments from the cove: that gunshot's first crack; the burning tire; the sight of Samson's open jaws. Doped up as I was on drugs, I had a hard time distinguishing reality from delusion. Once, late at night, I swore I heard Daniel singing, but when I looked around, the dark room was empty.

When I finally came to for good, groggy and confused in the early morning light, my mother was sitting in a chair in the corner, paging through her worn Bible. The mattress was propped up just a little, so I could see her without lifting my head from the pillow, and she didn't notice my open eyes. I didn't speak, partly because I wanted to be sure this wasn't another dream, partly because I couldn't think of what to say. I didn't know if Daniel was alive or dead, and I was afraid to ask. His beating heart, the last thing I could recall, seemed more fantasy than memory.

My mother's face was gaunt, as if she'd gone days without food or sleep, and I could tell too that she'd been crying. Rather than deal with her pain and my own, I closed my eyes and slipped back into the haze.

Later — a couple hours? The next morning? — I opened my eyes again and saw the television was on. Just past the foot of the bed, high up on the wall, a cartoon turtle walked beside a cartoon moose with a red bow tie. There was no sound, and the blocky letters of the closed captioning sputtered across the bottom of the screen. My mother sat in her chair, Bible on her lap, head tilted in sleep. My eyes rolled away from her and settled on the bottom of my bed. In the space where the lower half of my right leg should have been, there was nothing but a flat white sheet. I saw the peak made by my left foot and moved it, making the sheet ripple. But when I thought, *Right foot, move*, nothing happened, because it simply wasn't there. This was impossible, of course, and even after I reached down, even after my hand under the sheet gingerly touched the gauze-covered stump that ended just past the knee, the amputation didn't seem real. Nothing seemed real.

The Bible thumped to the floor and I turned to my mother, who had stood up but not rushed over. She crossed the room slowly, came to my side, and put two hands on my arm. "Thank God you came back," she said. "Oh, my sweet girl."

That's what she called me when I was little. She leaned in over the IV tubing and kissed my cheek. "The surgeons didn't have a choice," she said. "Your leg, it was just too —"

Samson's open jaw flashed in my mind. "So they just cut it off?"

She shook her head. "They tried their best, Annie. They saved as much as they could. Things were worse than you know." She clutched at her mouth, as if the words themselves scared her. When she took her hands away, she said, "They kept telling me you'd wake up, but it's been three days."

Three days, I thought. I wondered again about Daniel, a subject my mother was clearly avoiding. She went on. "I've already talked with the doctors about your recovery. They say with time and effort, you'll still be able to have a perfectly normal life."

"A perfectly normal life!" I shouted back at her. "Sure. Of course. Me and my freaking peg leg. That's exactly what we'll have." Tears pressed in along the rims of my eyes. I was trapped in that bed. I couldn't stop looking at the place where my leg should've been, though the sight disgusted me. I turned away from the stump, turned away from my mother, and finally fixed on the TV, where the cartoon moose was spinning that turtle on its back.

"Annie," my mother said. "They had to do this. They did it to save your life."

Something in the way she said this made me feel like I should be grateful, like not everyone got to live through what happened. My brother. That twisted neck and his still chest. I wondered if Jeff had told her about the hoax or if she thought I'd killed Daniel while trying to steal him from her. How do you apologize to a mother for a thing like that? How could I apologize for all I'd put her through? The tears seeped out now, just a few from both eyes. I wiped my cheeks and tried to find better words, but all I could come up with were the same ones we always use. "I'm so sorry, Mom." My voice was scratchy and raw. "They should have let me die."

"Don't you worry about being sorry," my mom said. "You worry about getting well." She poured some water from a pitcher into a cup, and I sipped it through a bent straw while she watched. She had no reason to offer such quick forgiveness. When I finished, she took the cup back. "Everyone has been praying."

I sniffled back the tears, made them stop, and focused on the Bible she'd been reading, still spread on the floor. "Don't tell me you believe this was all part of God's plan."

"What I think isn't relevant. Everything is a part of God's plan."

"Dad leaving?" I said. I rubbed the last of the wetness from my eyes. "What happened to Daniel?"

"All of it," she said. "The good and the bad. The things we understand and especially the things we don't."

"Oh, there's plenty I don't understand," I said. Why my leg was gone. Why Daniel had to die. But also, I remembered now, the scent of vanilla and that swirling white warmth from the cove. On the TV, the moose and turtle began dancing. The closed captioning read HAPPY MUSIC. "Can you please turn that crap off?" I said.

"Of course," my mom said. She lifted the remote from a chair next to the bed and tried to find the right button. "Daniel must have left it on."

"Daniel?" I said.

And at that moment my brother walked into the room, his arm in a cast up past his elbow, the whole thing suspended in a blue sling. "Hey, Andi," he said. "You're awake." A square white bandage covered half his forehead. He crossed to my mother and handed her a Crunch bar. He said, "I told you Andi was gonna be okay."

She gave him back the unwrapped chocolate and said, "You sure did."

Daniel offered me the candy bar and I hesitated, then took a bite. "Thanks," I told him, still not believing my eyes.

He said, "Mom says you're gonna get a wheelchair till you get a new leg. Can I have a ride?"

Mom shushed him, but Daniel didn't care. He waited for an answer to his question with a beaming smile on his face. I was shocked to hear myself laugh. "Yeah, sure thing," I told him. "You're first in line." I gave him back his candy bar and looked at the bandage on his head. I wondered what he remembered about the cove. "Daniel, how do you feel?"

"I have a compound fracture," he announced proudly. "I'm glad you're awake. I couldn't read them words fast enough." Now he was looking again at the TV screen, munching his chocolate.

"We should call the doctors, Annie," my mom said. "They'll want to know you're awake. But first things first." She turned off the TV. "Let's pray now, the three of us."

Daniel put down the candy bar, folded his hands, and bent his head reverently. My mom looked at me, waiting. I stared down, expecting still to see my right leg just as it had always been. Instead, there was only the clean white sheet covering the stump. But I also remembered that warmth within my chest, the glowing that filled my whole body.

"How about you guys pray, and I'll listen?" I said.

Mom held back her smile, but I could tell she was pleased. She closed her eyes and began. She didn't ask God to straighten the path before me, and she didn't ask Him to take away my pain. That day, all she focused on was offering thanks for sparing my life. I let my eyes close, leaned back into the pillow, and listened to the words of my mother's prayer.

• • •

That first day in the hospital, a doctor came in and explained that during surgery I'd gone into septic shock. Technically I'd been in a coma. He asked how my pain was on a scale of one to ten. I couldn't pick a number, so I told him four. Another doctor, this one a lady, pulled a chair up close to the bed and explained the lengthy rehab she had planned out for me. Later a counselor stopped by and said we should talk sometime about mourning my missing leg. It all seemed crazy, impossible, wrong. Yet all this time, while the images of crutches and wheelchairs and metal joints strapped to my flesh made me cringe, I'd see my brother in the corner, reading a comic book, or at the window, smiling at a squirrel balancing along the telephone wire. Every time I felt like screaming or crying, I'd remember that strange warmth in my chest and think, *Daniel's alive.*

That night, after the parade of doctors finally stopped, after my mom and Daniel left for the hotel they were staying in, I fell into a deep sleep. I dreamt, but not about fire or Samson or the fairy fort. I dreamt I was running. On strong and powerful legs, I jogged across a never-ending green field with the open sky overhead. The wind flowed through my hair and I could run forever, it seemed, but then I was distracted by the sound of gentle weeping.

I opened my eyes in darkness and clicked on the little light on the nightstand. Leo was kneeling next to my bed. He had his head down, and he gripped the metal rail with both his hands, like he was holding on to keep from collapsing. When he raised his head, the sight of tears on that ravaged face was more than I wanted to see. He said, "Oh, Anderson, I am so sorry. I am so sorry for what's happened."

"You got nothing to apologize for," I said.

"I'm not convinced of that. It was I who called Daniel to the fairy fort."

"Nobody made me do anything," I told him. "I wanted to come. And so did Daniel."

With the back of his damaged hand, he wiped the tears from his face. "I came here tonight to receive your judgment. I came to ask you to forgive me."

I shrugged my shoulders. "Poof. You're forgiven."

He seemed shocked. His stare turned to the bottom of the bed. "But your leg," he said.

Given what Leo knew, it made no sense that I'd be so willing to offer absolution. What happened to my leg was a shitty deal, one I still cope with to this day. But losing it to save Daniel was a bargain I would've gladly accepted on those rocks. With as honest and good as Leo had been to me, and as terrible as he was clearly feeling, I thought he had a right to know. I started the story without even thinking. "That bear would've killed me for sure," I said. "But Daniel came back."

I explained how I'd gotten my brother to safety and how he returned from the lake. I told him about the pain and the blood and Bundower's sniper shots. And then, after I gathered myself, I told him how I found Daniel like I did, dying or dead already, with neither breath nor beating heart. I looked into Leo's ruined face and described what happened next as best as I could, how I broke my vow and asked for God's help. I finished my story and shrugged. "I'm not even sure what I did qualifies as a prayer," I said.

Leo was silent for a time. Then he said, "That's probably the best prayer I ever heard."

"It was so strange, though," I said. "There was this glowing inside me. It felt so warm, like it was almost alive."

"It was," Leo said. He smiled and nodded. "It most definitely was."

I shook my head. "I can't be sure God brought Daniel back from the dead. For all I know, Daniel's heart could've kicked back on all by itself. How can I be positive?"

"And where is it written God wants you to be certain?"

"I don't understand," I said.

"Faith isn't about absolute proof. Belief isn't a math problem. You prayed for your brother, Anderson. That's the truly miraculous act here, not what happened before or after. In your hour of need, when you had every reason to despair, you chose to reach out to God."

"But if He really heard me, why am I still alive at all? I offered my life for Daniel's."

Leo patted my arm. "I don't think God bargains like that. Besides, God may have needed you alive for a reason. He may have work He wants you to do."

I wasn't sure how I felt about doing God's work and gave Leo a look that demanded an explanation.

He smiled at me strangely. "You have seen astounding things, Anderson, but seeing alone merely makes you an observer. To be a witness, you must tell others what you saw. When the time is right, you must offer testimony. Make others feel what it felt like to be where you were. Tell your truth, Anderson Grant."

That last notion appealed to me, but I knew I wasn't ready,

not that night for sure. So we talked for a while about Daniel and what a great kid he was. It's funny, but I have no memory of Leo leaving. He slipped out after I fell asleep, and I never heard from him again.

The year since then has been anything but easy. I went from the trauma center to Good Shepherd Rehab in Allentown for the hardest six weeks of my life. I got fitted with a temporary leg, and they worked me out of the wheelchair, up into a walker like old folks use, then onto wobbly crutches. I practiced falling and getting up. I had to learn how to walk again, how to deal with stairs, get in and out of tubs, a dozen daily habits you just take for granted. Then Mom drove me back home, where I found Bundower and Jeff had moved all my stuff from my cabin to my old bedroom, given the walls a fresh coat of blue paint.

All winter, I was desperate to run, and I spent plenty of afternoons feeling sorry for myself. But when the snow wasn't bad, Daniel and I took longer and longer walks, and Gayle got in the habit of giving me rides in to the office even when she didn't need help. By spring, I had fixed up that bike in the shed and, with some practice, rode it along Roosevelt Road, pretending I was jogging. A couple times a week, Jeff called from Penn State to check in and razz me about how when I get to campus in the fall, he'll be a senior and I'll only be a freshman. Little by little, my new life started taking shape.

At nine months, my stump had matured and I got fitted for a permanent prosthetic, which was more comfortable but still no good for real running. A bunch of folks around town — Gayle and Bundower, Mayor Wheeler and even the Abernathys — they all pitched in and sent me to see a specialist in New York. My running leg's lighter and got more flexibility; there's a bowed metal blade where you'd expect a stiff rod. Sticking to the roads, I've worked my way up to looping the lake, though my time still sucks. This summer, when Jeff runs with me, he's got to hold back. For now.

Some days my leg still hurts, or I get an itch on the bottom of that long-gone foot. And I still have nights when I wake up sweating in the cove, or when I reach for that knee, screaming in my sleep. But out on the road with the wind whipping through my hair, I get that old sensation of freedom and lightness that comes with speed, the thrill that accompanies motion. I just like feeling like I'm going somewhere.

As for the Pilgrims and the true believers, they kind of faded away after the accident. Gayle told me Leo stepped in right away, urging the believers to let my family heal and look elsewhere for their miracles. My mom stopped bringing Daniel to the UCP, and everybody around town, even Volpe and the Abernathys, refused to talk to the few reporters who called. Scarecrow, who kept ranting about God's voice and "testing" Daniel, went straight from the fairy fort to Bundower's jail and then got shipped to Bonneville, a place with walled gardens and bars on the windows. Gayle put that story on the front page. Bundower, from what I hear, made it clear to the citizens of Paradise that Daniel was to be left alone. Everybody could see how close he and my mom were getting, and folks weren't eager to cross him.

These days, nobody comes right out and asks Daniel to pray. Being Daniel, I know he wouldn't mind, but I don't think he misses the pressure of being the Miracle Boy. I've never asked him what he remembers about the cove, if he recalls saving me by taming Samson or a white tunnel of light. But sometimes when he thinks I'm not watching, I catch Daniel staring at me. In these moments, I turn to my brother, and he smiles like he knows a pretty good secret.

It took me a good long while to come to terms and feel ready, but I've tried here to be faithful to Leo's calling, to be a witness to what happened to Daniel and me. And you're probably wondering after all this, what do I believe? That's a fair question. Is there a benevolent divine being watching over us all with a plan for our lives, waiting to intervene with miraculous acts? *Of course,* my mom would certainly answer, and once this would've been a no-brainer for me too. But after Daniel fell in that hole, after my father left us and the town seemed to die and everything went crazy, I would've told you, *Not a chance.* I can't deny, though, the things I saw later eroded my bitterness — that Abernathy baby, the faces of those people lined up in the fairy fort, the way Daniel came back for me. In the end, I guess, out on the jagged rocks of McGinley's Cove, I gave up my anger for something better. To this day, it's not something I'd call faith exactly, but something closer to hope. I'll never be a Holy Roller nutjob. I'm just more open to things I don't understand, the mysterious possibilities around us all. So here's my grand answer: *Maybe.* This might come across as some lame cop-out, but for me — a daddy's girl abandoned by her father, a big sister who nearly killed her kid brother, a born runner who lost a leg — it seems honest, sincere, even hopeful. *Maybe* feels like a prayer all its own.

AUTHOR'S NOTE

While there is indeed an actual Paradise, Pennsylvania, it has no bearing on the fictional place of the same name in this book. I created this Paradise, as well as its geography and all its inhabitants, entirely from my imagination. Any resemblance to the real Paradise or its citizens is strictly coincidental. As for my iron-willed main character and her potential similarity to my eight older sisters, I have no comment.

I'd like to express my deepest gratitude to several folks who saved this manuscript from certain death. I thank George Clark, for his enthusiasm and expertise on fairy forts. I thank Warren Frazier, for his always thoughtful criticism and guidance. And I thank editor Cheryl Klein, who would likely be unbearable if she weren't right so often. Her belief in Andi made all the difference.

For their camaraderie and inspiration, I thank my colleagues at McNeese State and the many graduate writers who have made up the MFA workshop I'm so privileged to be a part of.

Lastly, it is impossible to imagine any part of my life without Beth. For all our renaissances, and the ones that await us still, I am endlessly grateful.

This book was edited by Cheryl Klein and designed by Christopher Stengel. The text was set in Dante, with display type set in Adrianna. This book was printed and bound by R. R. Donnelley in Crawfordsville, Indiana. The production was supervised by Cheryl Weisman. The manufacturing was supervised by Jess White.